GHOSTED

EXPERIMENT IN TERROR #9.5

KARINA HALLE

For my Dex

FOREWORD

Ghosted was originally published in the All the Love the World Anthology. While it's a novella (told in Dex's POV), it's important that it be read after Veiled and before Came Back Haunted. The last book in the EIT series before this was Dust to Dust #9, however Ghosted takes place after Veiled (the EIT spinoff about Ada), so it makes sense to read it after Veiled.

Came Back Haunted picks up where this story left off, so strap yourself in and get ready for the return of Dex and Perry!

ONE

"Excuse me, are you Dex Foray?"

I stop in my tracks as I'm walking past the Chief of Seattle statue in Tilikum Place, and look over my shoulder at a Danny Devito-sized man hurrying toward me, clutching an oversized trench coat around him that flaps in the cold breeze. Can't pretend I didn't see the man loitering outside of the apartment moments earlier, having followed me down the block. Of course, with my fucking luck, this is the type of stalker I get.

"You don't know me," he says breathlessly, his voice coarse and nasal. He holds out one hand while trying to keep his coat closed with the other. "I'm Harry. Harry Cox."

Don't laugh. Don't fucking laugh.

I bite back a grin, and turn around, staring at his hand for a moment before I give a hesitant shake. It's small, chubby, clammy. I imagine it's like shaking hands with a starfish.

"How do you know who I am?" I ask him, just as the wind whips a fallen yellow leaf into his face, sticking to his black-rimmed glasses. "Better yet, how did you know where I live?"

He reaches up and hastily wipes the leaf away.

"Your address is on your website. I've been trying to reach you for a long time," he says, giving me an apologetic smile. I'm a pro at reading people's energies these days, more than I want to be, and this guy is anxious as fuck, which in turn sets me on edge. "But all my emails have gone unanswered. I've left some messages too."

"With who?"

"With *whom*," the man corrects me, and what a fucking dickladle this guy is. "I don't know. I used the contact form through your website and I've left a few messages on your voicemail."

"My wife handles those," I tell him, folding my arms across my chest. Perry runs a pretty tight ship when it comes to managing Haunted Media, our video production company, so it surprises me that she'd drop the ball with this guy. "And you're what, a band manager?" I squint at his attire. "Accountant?"

"As I've said on my many voice messages and emails," he says, his voice growing a pitch higher, "I'm not interested in your video services. I'm interested in your *other* services."

I frown. Like...sexually?

I raise my brow. "Well, Mr., uh, Cox. I'm afraid I have no idea what you're talking about. We run a studio, primarily for music video production. We don't have any other type of business. Or services. Of *any* kind. And if you don't mind, I need to pick up my pizza before it gets cold." I jerk my head toward Zeek's, our local pizza parlor, before heading down the street toward it.

"Experiment in Terror," he calls out from behind me.

I stop.

He walks around me, getting between me and the pizza place. "I need *those* services."

I blink at him, trying to figure him out. His anxiety is still through the roof, but it's coupled with something else. Desperation. It rises out of him, like steam from a turd. A most unsettling image.

"We don't...you know that was just a show, right?"

"You saw those ghosts. I know they were real," he says, his eyes sparking beneath his glasses. "I know they're real too. That the monsters really do live under our beds."

Okay, now he's looking a tad erratic. I can't say that Perry and I don't get stopped on the street from time to time by people who were fans of EIT, asking us if we're going to do another episode, grilling us about what was real, or just wanting a lame-ass photo. But this guy...this guy's not like them.

"Look, Mr. Cox, I don't understand what this is about," I tell him firmly. "Whether what we filmed was real or not, that's all done with. It's over. We haven't filmed a show in over three years."

"But you talk to the dead!" he cries out, loud enough that the people walking past us on street pause, give us a funny look. "That can't just go away. That's in you. That stays in you."

I stare at him for a moment, wondering if he's about to go a little fucknuts on me. I know crazy, believe me, and he's walking a fine line here.

"It doesn't go away," I tell him carefully, though I'm not sure why I'm being honest with someone I don't know. "That's the truth. And that's one reason out of many why we don't do the show anymore. We wanted to leave that chapter behind, if we could help it. Now, I'm sorry, but—"

"My wife died," he says softly, grabbing at his glasses

with fumbling fingers and quickly wiping his eyes. He inhales sharply, slips the glasses back on. "She died. A year ago. I need you to talk to her. I know she's still in the house."

I swallow, now picking up on his sorrow. It's overwhelming.

"I'm sorry," I tell him, trying to distance myself from his emotions, which ripple through the air. "How did she die?"

"She...drowned."

"And she's still in your house?"

"She's in *the* house. Our old house. I don't live there anymore. It's boarded up."

"Listen, I'm not a paranormal investigator. I never was. Maybe a paranormal shit-disturber, at best."

"You can see things that others can't."

"Doesn't mean I'm a medium."

"Your wife is."

I frown at him, tilting my head, a thread of defensiveness running through me whenever Perry is mentioned. "How would you know that?"

He shrugs. "I've seen the footage."

"You're making an awful lot of assumptions from some grainy videos," I tell him. "She's not any of those things either. We're just two people who went through some crazy fucking shit, who are trying to lead an ordinary life. Now, if you'll excuse me, I really have to go."

I turn to leave but the man reaches out and grabs my forearm, hard.

A current of anger flows through me and I have to breathe in sharply to keep it at bay. I don't appreciate being manhandled on the street by low-rent Danny Devito and his tiny baby hands.

"I'll pay you," he says. "I'll pay you a lot of money. I just want you to come by, the both of you, go to the house, and talk to her. You don't have to film it. I just want to know what my wife has to say. I have questions. I need answers."

I rip my arm out of his grasp and take a step back. "How much money?"

The man looks around us, as if he's finally getting the clue that he should have kept his voice down this whole time. He leans in to me. "A hundred grand."

I blink at him. "Excuse me?"

"Yeah. A hundred grand. I'll write you a check right now."

He starts reaching into his coat and the movement snaps me out of my daze.

"Hold on, wait a minute," I say, raising my hands, trying to think.

Is he fucking serious?

A hundred grand?

Just to attempt to talk to his dead wife?

I hate the way my heart is beating fast at the thought of a hundred thousand dollars and how many fucking problems that would solve for us.

"I know what you're thinking," he says quickly. "That it's a lot of money."

"Fucking hell it's a shitton of money. How would you even—"

"I have money," he says quickly. "Don't worry about that. It's legitimate. It's worth it to me."

I shake my head, knowing there's a catch.

"Let me get this straight, before my mind starts running away on me. You want to give me and my wife one hundred thousand dollars to go into your old house and talk to your dead wife? What if we can't make contact? What if nothing happens?"

"Then you keep the money," he says gravely. "It will be worth it just to see you try."

Worth it? There's no way I could keep the money if we were unsuccessful. I mean, I'm no saint, of course I would be tempted, but I'm pretty sure Perry would refuse. Hell, she might refuse this idea at any rate.

"I'm going to have to think about it," I say after a moment.

"You think about it," he says. "But it's Halloween in a couple of days and I've been doing my research. I think that's when you should do it. That's when it's easier to communicate with spirits, where the Veil is thin. The witches call it Samhain."

"Uh huh," I say carefully, running my hand over the stubble on my chin. I'm not exactly how true that is since the two of us have tussled with the dead and undead on ordinary Tuesdays. Plus, we already have plans on Halloween. "I'll see what Perry says."

"Please do," he says. He reaches into his pocket and hands me his business card.

Harry Cox.

Accountant.

"I knew it," I mutter under my breath. The guy has numbers dweeb written all over him.

"Not for a band. Just an ordinary accountant, I'm afraid."

"An ordinary accountant with a hundred grand to spare?" I raise my brow.

He gives me a curt nod, quickly ties his coat shut over his rotund belly, and then says, "I really hope I'll be hearing from you, Mr. Foray."

And then he turns around and disappears down Cedar Street past the 5 Point Café. I watch him for a moment, then almost head back to the apartment until I remember the pizza and the fact that Perry would kill me if I didn't come back with our dinner. I don't think any amount of money would suffice her *hanger*.

I grab the pizza from Zeek's, and then head back down the street, walking alongside the monorail and back to our building

When I walk inside our apartment, Perry's leaning against the island in the kitchen, her dark hair flowing around her face, blue eyes wild with hunger.

"What took you so long?" she asks, practically ripping the pizza box out of my hands.

"I ran into someone," I tell her, grabbing the plates from the cupboard and placing them on the counter.

"Uh huh," she says, shoving a pizza slice in her mouth. Her eyes fall close with pleasure as she chews, which makes me smile. She has a strained relationship with food sometimes, so to see her enjoy it so hedonistically is a relief.

Okay, it's also a bit of a turn-on.

"Aren't you curious who?" I ask, pulling a slice toward me and sitting down on the stool. "Or *whom*." That fucker.

She finishes chewing, swallows, and looks at me with her full attention. "Yes."

"Harry Cox." I can't help but snicker as I say it.

Perry, however, isn't smiling. "What?"

"I take it you've heard of him? Least that's what he told me."

She frowns. "How did he find you?"

"Our address is on the website. Is there a reason you didn't tell me about him?"

She sighs heavily and looks away, worry on her brow. "Because the man is a joke."

"Is he now? What makes you say that?"

She gives me a sharp look. "If you met him, I'm sure he told you what he's been emailing and calling me about."

"Emailing and calling *us*. This is an us, kiddo. We're a team here. You should have told me. You know nothing good comes from keeping secrets." I pause, biting my lip. "It's not exactly fair that you can access my mind anytime you want but I'm often shut out of yours."

She rolls her eyes. "You know it doesn't work that way."

Yeah, yeah. She says that all the time. It's her go-to excuse, but I know that since she has the ability to read minds at will (not everyone's mind, and not always very clearly), it's made our marriage a little one-sided at times.

"Anyway," she continues, "you can pick up on feelings and energies. It's pretty much the same."

"It is very much *not* the same. If I meet someone and they're giving off the vibes that they're afraid of me, the buck stops there. I don't know *why* they're afraid of me. I just know that they are. But you do."

"It's because you're a weirdo," she says with a smirk.

"I'm not asking you why they're afraid of me. Anyway, point being...you're the fucking weirdo here."

She laughs and then grows serious, her gaze sharpening. "Back to Mr. Cox."

"Really? You're not going to use his full name? Cheap laughs may be cheap, but they count."

I can tell by her steely gaze she's not finding me very amusing at the moment, nor the name of Harry Cox.

"What did he want?" she asks.

"For us to go into his old boarded-up haunted house and have a fucking séance with his dead wife."

She presses her lips together into a thin line. I already know that it's going to be an uphill battle to even get her to consider this. Hell, I can't blame her. It was absolutely out of the question until Mr. Dick started waving his check book around.

"And you wondered why I didn't pass the messages along?" she asks, reaching for another slice of pizza.

"Did he tell you he wants to pay us?"

Her hand freezes in mid-air, her eyes flitting up to mine. "No."

I grab her hand and hold it, giving it a squeeze. "He wants to pay us a lot of money to do this. I know it sounds fucking ridiculous, the whole being paid a bunch of money to spend a night in a haunted house, but that's pretty much the deal."

"How much money is a bunch of money?"

"A hundred grand."

Her hand goes limp in mine, her mouth gaping. "What?" She takes her hand back, eyes round. "A hundred grand?"

I nod. "That's what he said."

"And you believe him?"

"I think so. The man is desperate, Perry."

She continues to stare at me, dumbfounded. "That... none of this makes any sense."

"For what it's worth, I didn't get the impression he was lying or trying to fuck us over. I don't know, I'm sure you can get a better read on him and find out the truth, but I have to say, I think he's damn serious."

"It's a trap."

"How so?"

"I don't know. Why would anyone have that much money to give?"

"I don't think it really matters."

"Well, what does he do?"

"He's an accountant."

She laughs in disbelief. "An accountant? What does he do, launder money for a drug cartel? This isn't *Ozark*."

"Maybe he does. Either way, it's a hundred fucking grand. This would change our whole life, Perry."

Her jaw tenses and she straightens up, leaning on the counter. "You're seriously considering this?"

"You're seriously not?" I throw my hands out. "Do you not realize what that money can do for us?"

"Do you not realize that this could destroy us?!" Her voice is high, shrill, and there's fear washing over her, radiating outward like a tidal wave.

Fuck.

"Baby," I say to her quietly, feeling every cell inside me soften. I go over around the island and grab her hands, holding them up and pressing them against my chest. "Talk to me. Talk me through this. What's going on in that head of yours?"

"Why do you even have to ask?" she says softly.

"Because that's how we communicate. Please don't expect me to read your mind, because I can't."

"You're asking me to step into that world again."

"I'm not asking anything of you yet, just to listen, just to consider it."

"You don't get it, do you?"

Her words slice me. Usually Perry is pretty even keeled, except when she's PMSing (and I know better than to ever admit that out loud to her), but for the past few weeks she's been on edge. I've been waiting for her to tell me and talk to me about it, but I suppose that's a conversation for another time.

"Explain," I say patiently.

She shakes her head and I know she's about to pull

away, but I press her hands against me tighter. She's not going anywhere, and she knows it.

"Things have been pretty good, haven't they?" she asks, her eyes searching mine. "It's been three years and six months since I lost my mother, and every day is a new step forward, walking out of those ashes. I'm married to my best friend, whom I am still deeply in love with, we have a successful company. We have good friends in a city that's been good to us. My father finally seems to be...moving on. Or he's at least trying to. My sister..." she trails off and shakes her head, blinking. "Well, that just proves my point doesn't it? We're doing okay only because we left the fucked-up paranormal world behind."

"This isn't EIT," I tell her. "This is something else entirely. You told me that you'd one day want to talk to ghosts instead of screaming and running from them."

"No," she says, taking her hands away and putting them on her hips, her saucy Italian side coming out. "*You* said that we could become paranormal investigators like the Warrens. That was never my idea. And I believe I said I'd file it as a to-do in five years. It's been three."

"But what's the harm in doing it once?"

Her eyes nearly bug-out. "What's the harm? Dex, what did I just say? Things have been good because we're not dealing with the dead. We're not seeking shit out. Ada's life is all over the place now that she's got Jay and can see demons and whatever the fuck. That's bad enough as it is, do you really want that for us?"

"This would be different. This man is asking us to talk to his dead wife. Don't you feel for him? Don't you want to help? You have a gift Perry, why can't you use it for good?"

"Nice, Dex, you're trying to guilt me now. Why are you so insistent on this?"

"I'm not, I just want you to look at our options. This is a good opportunity."

Her eyes narrow at me for a moment. "You know who you sound like right now?"

I stare at her. "Who?"

"You. The Dex from day one, when I ran into you in that lighthouse. That's who you sound like. Opportunistic, not giving a shit why I'm putting my foot down, forever forcing me to do something I don't want to do, something I know is a bad idea."

I cock my head as I stare at her, my pulse picking up in my throat. "Are we fighting here?"

"Maybe," she says with a sigh, running her hand down her face. "Look, I get that it's a lot of money, but there's just too much risk."

"You won't even think about it?"

She turns and walks over to the window, passing by our Frenchie, Fat Rabbit, who is sleeping on the couch. The fat pooch sleeps through everything, and since our personalities have always been combative, the dog is used to this kind of shit with us. Okay, maybe it's not fair to say we're both combative. I'm usually the problem and I've gotten pretty good at pushing her buttons...in more ways than one.

Perry exhales and leans against the windowsill, staring out at the Seattle skyline as it grows darker and darker with the coming evening.

I follow her. I know I should give her a lot of space, especially when she's been so prickly and emotional lately, but, like I said, button-pusher.

"Baby," I tell her softly, placing my hands on her shoulders. "We could do so much. We could sell this place, buy a house. A real proper house where there isn't a monorail chugging past us all day long, where there's a yard for Fat

Rabbit. We can finally get another dog, the fat gray pit bull you want to adopt. Remember? You want to call it Lil Hippo. Lil Hippo and Fatty Rab can run around the yard. We can have peace and space and…" I want to tell her we could have space for a baby, but that's a topic we don't discuss anymore. "We could have enough for a house on the Sound. We could revitalize the business."

I could film my documentary…

I feel her relaxing under my palms. "It really would fix a lot of problems, wouldn't it?"

"I just want you to think about it," I tell her softly, kissing the back of her head, breathing in the tropical-scent of her shampoo, a smell that feels like home to me. "I'll never make you do anything you don't want to do. I'm not that guy anymore."

She lets out a light snort. "That guy is still in you, Dex. Maybe a little older now, a little more subdued. And, really, you never forced me to do anything. It's just that you're extremely persuasive."

"I'd say my dick drives a hard bargain, but that was before I was screwing you."

She leans back against my hands, sighing. "That it does." She turns her head to glance up at me over her shoulder. "I'll think about it. But no promises."

TWO

"Happy anniversary," Perry whispers into my ear.

Before I even have time to fully wake-up and register what's happening, I feel her warm hand slip underneath the covers and wrap around the hard length of my perpetual morning wood.

"Happy anniversary to you too," I manage to say through a groan, my eyes fluttering open. My head rolls to the side and I focus on her face in the morning light of our bedroom. Fucking hell, it doesn't matter that I met her four years ago, or that we were married three years ago—my wife never fails to take my breath away.

Especially when she's holding onto my cock.

"I know tonight isn't exactly the anniversary that you hoped for," she says, biting on her full lower lip for a moment, mischief sparkling in her eyes. This morning they're the color of the ocean on a cloudy day. "But I figured I could at least get your morning off to a great start."

"You won't hear me complaining," I tell her, my heart rate picking up as she climbs over me, her hair falling over her face and tickling my bare chest. Though I sleep nude, she's always wearing some old threadbare concert tee, and while she looks phenomenally hot in them, there's nothing like feeling her bare skin first thing in the morning.

I reach down and try to remove her shirt, but she just gives me a wicked smile.

"Nope," she says, trailing her fingers over my chest, over the words tattooed there, *And With Madness Comes the Light.* "This is all for you. The least I can do for making you have dinner with my dad on our anniversary."

"Uh, if you could not mention your father when you're about to suck me off, that would be great."

"Sorry," she says sweetly, so sweet that it borders on sarcastic. Makes me want to flip her over and spank her ass a few times.

But she has other plans, leaving hot, wet kisses down the middle of my abs, lower and lower. I'm already tense, hard as fucking cement. She disappears under the covers and I quickly lift them up, not wanting to miss a single second of this show. It's not that we don't have a healthy sex life for a married couple, but it's also not every day that she wakes me up with a blow job.

I watch as she slides her fist down my shaft, her eyes glued to mine. Her mouth parts, and she licks the rim of her bottom lip.

Dex, you lucky piece of shit.

I don't know what I did to deserve this woman, but she's here, she's slipping the swollen tip of my dick between her lips, and I completely surrender to her.

I always have.

"Fuck me," I whisper, my voice already ragged as she sucks at me, her tongue swirling around until I can no longer hold eye contact. My head flops back against the pillow and I'm not ashamed to admit I'm not going to last that long. My wife has skills that run deep, and she plays it fast and furious.

My eyes roll back in my head, tension threading through me, coiling in my stomach. Instinctively I reach for her hair, wrapping my fingers around her strands, tugging hard. She brings me in deeper, her fingers working my balls, doing everything as only she knows how.

"Christ, Perry," I grunt, yanking at her hair, wanting nothing more than to come. "You're asking for trouble if you keep that going."

I feel her mouth widen into a smile before her fist grips me harder, tighter, moving faster. The pressure inside me builds until the dam is unleashed.

I groan loudly, the sound thunderous in the bedroom, heat snaking down my spine until I feel ripped apart. I come inside her throat, my hips bucking up against her mouth, hands tangled in her hair.

Fucking fuck.

I'm left gasping on the bed, my limbs weightless, my soul circling around for a moment before it returns.

"You," I manage to say, my voice hoarse. I lift my head and gaze at Perry, who looks extremely satisfied with herself. She wipes her lips slowly, her chin wet, and I know if I hadn't just come so fucking hard I'd be turned on all over again. "You have a fucking gift, you know that?"

Her brows raise, cheeks flushed against her pale skin. "Seems I do."

"I wouldn't mind waking up like that every day for the next three years, just saying."

She laughs as she sits up, smacking my chest playfully. "Don't be greedy, Dex." She moves to the edge of the bed.

"Where are you going?" I make a grab for her, but she's quick.

"To get ready," she says, stepping out of my grasp. "I don't want to rush us, but I told my father we'd be there by three and I've got some work I need to do before then."

She goes to the bathroom, closing the door behind her, and I sigh, collapsing back into the bed.

So, today is our wedding anniversary. Three years. Not a huge number, and apparently not a big deal when it comes to the gold, silver, bronze—whatever other Olympic medals there are for surviving marriage. But still, every year is special and poignant and for whatever reason, Perry decided we should celebrate with her father and sister.

I mean, I get it. Even though Perry said she's been stepping forward after her mother's death, the family has had a lot of setbacks and she needs to be with them often, propelled by guilt. Her father still hasn't dated anyone, and tends to keep to himself. She's often mentioned that he seems to have lost his faith, which isn't great for a theology professor.

Then there's her nineteen-year old sister, Ada, who, in the last year, has discovered she has a lot of the same abilities as Perry, enough so that she has her very own guardian douchebag. She also went to Hell to rescue their mother. Literal Hell. Ever since then, well, she's grown up extremely fast, and even though she's in Instagram college or something, seeing ghosts and demons has been a bit of a struggle for her.

And Perry, well...she puts on a sunny face, but since her thoughts sometimes leak out to me, never mind her emotions, I know that things are hard. She says she's been happier since she put the show behind her, and I think she's right about that. But I know she still carries a lot of fear with her.

Because the thing is, losing your mother isn't something you just grow out of.

I should know.

And neither is seeing ghosts.

Or having the ability to read minds.

Or creating portals to another dimension out of thin air.

I know Perry still sees things she pretends not to see. I can't blame her for acting like she doesn't. Fuck, that's how I operated for most of my life. Her solution, the way she's adapted to try and be normal, to just survive, is to look the other way and pretend it's not happening.

I should understand this. But deep down, in my gut, it worries me.

These things, this other world…it *wants* you to look at it.

And I'm afraid that it will get angrier the more we ignore it.

There're so few who are able to do what we do. People say they want to explore the unknown, to stare into the abyss and have that fucking abyss stare right back at you.

In reality though, they'll always turn and run away with their tail between their legs. Very few people have the stomach to face the things that scare them.

That's one reason why I think taking up Mr. Cox on his offer might make a lot of sense. There is no fear here. This is a desperate man who lost his wife, who will do anything to connect with her.

If I put myself in his position, I know I'd give all the money in the world to hear from Perry again. I'd do anything. Give my own life if it could save hers.

I've done it before.

And this time, it's not exploitive. We could actually help someone. We could be in control. We could communicate with this woman and unite her with her lost loved one.

We could make a real difference in the lives of the living and the dead.

And it would let Perry know that there's nothing to fear here.

The past is behind us.

So are the people we were.

But we're in control of the people that we can be.

It starts with facing our fears.

Naturally, a hundred grand comes along for the ride, just to sweeten the pot.

But money or no money, I know I've got my work cut out for me. Tomorrow is Halloween, and since we're spending tonight with her family in Portland, we're going to stay at a cabin on Cannon Beach tomorrow. Celebrating our wedding anniversary on Halloween felt fitting.

Yet, if tomorrow is supposed to be the best night to communicate with the dead, according to some witches or whatever, then it looks like our romantic getaway will have to be postponed.

Yeah. Perry is probably going to kill me if I push for this again.

Luckily, I know how to deal with her wrath.

THE DRIVE FROM SEATTLE TO PORTLAND IS USUALLY boring as shit, but this time it's a little more exciting, thanks to my Highlander's transmission problems when we stop for gas in Kelso. The car is usually reliable but this year it's started to show its age and I know it's only a matter of time before it starts to be a constant issue.

Thankfully I'm able to get it started after twenty

minutes fiddling with the engine, while Perry threatens to call roadside assistance and take away my man card.

"You know, with a hundred grand, we could trade this puppy in and get one of them new hybrids," I tell her once we're back on the road, smacking the wheel.

I can feel the spike of anger from her and I glance at her. She's all flinty-eyed.

"I thought we already discussed this," she says.

"No, you said you would think about it." I pause. "I know I've been thinking about it. A lot."

She worries her lip between her teeth and looks out the window. "It's a bad idea, Dex."

"Why?"

"I already told you why. Don't you listen to anything I say?"

I know it seems like I'm not listening, but I need to approach this whole thing from another angle.

"Let's pretend I'm a fuckwit and you need to explain yourself again."

She lets out a long, heavy sigh, putting her head briefly in her hands. "Fine. I don't want to because I'm scared. Okay? You happy now?"

"Happy that you're scared? No, baby. That doesn't make me very happy."

Honestly, I didn't expect her to just admit it like that. She's tough as shit and has been through so much, that it takes a lot for her to just be vulnerable, even with me, even after all this time.

We drive in silence for a few minutes. My mind is spinning over what she said. Even though I know facing her fears would be good for her, I could never put her in a position where she's admittedly scared.

Not for all the money in the world.

"I'm sorry," she says eventually.

"What for?"

"I know you really want this."

I lick my lips, trying to weigh my words carefully. "It's not that I really want this, Perry. I just...until you told me the truth, that you were scared, I just thought it was a good life-changing opportunity. It wasn't just about the money, even though that's a huge fucking part of it."

"So what else is it about?"

"It's like...you know, I like what I do, I like our company." I give her a quick smile. "*Love* our company. It's so very us and even though we're quite niche, we're able to make a living. It's the perfect combination of the two of us. But..."

"But what?" She's sitting up straighter, her eyes on me, bright and focused.

"I fucking hate to say this because it sounds ridiculous, but the two of us are special. I hate that word, hate it, but sometimes it makes sense. It does here. We're unique. We have an ability that so few have. Don't you think we're supposed to do something with it? I mean what's the fucking point of being able to see ghosts and travel through the Veil and talk to the dead if we're not going to use it?"

She swallows, blinks at me.

I grip the wheel tighter, feeling that fear seeping out from her.

"I'm just being honest," I tell her quickly. I give her an expectant look. "You know, once upon a time, that's all you ever wanted from me."

"I know when you're being honest and when you're not," she says slowly. "Doesn't mean I like to hear it."

"Well, you just told me you were scared, so don't worry. That trumps everything I just said."

I exhale, the silence between us growing louder. I'm

reaching for my phone to pick a playlist, when she grabs my hand, holding it tight.

"I love you, you know that," she says softly.

I don't know why every time I hear those words, my chest seizes, my stomach dips, like I'm hearing it again for the very first time. The intensity inside me, my feelings for her, they've only grown stronger over the years. Sometimes I find myself loving her so much that it scares me to my core. Maybe because in the back of my mind, there's always that fear that I won't have her forever. Deep down inside, I'm still that scared little boy that lost too much, too soon.

I've learned not to take things for granted. It's a survival mechanism.

I manage a smile. "I love you too, baby. You know I won't do anything that you don't want to do, and I'll never put you in the position where you'd be scared. Okay?"

"I know," she says. "I know that. And I know that this means something to you. That you want to use our gifts but...how does that lead to a happy ending for us? How does that not put us back in time, down a road of horror and sorrow and bad choices?"

"Because we're different people now."

"*You're* a different person. You have no fear because you can't die."

I let out a sharp laugh. "Hey, we agreed that we were never going to look at it like that. That only invites death, remember? I can die, I *have* died, lest you forgot that, and I can get hurt. To think otherwise is too damn dangerous."

"So how come you aren't scared?"

I shrug. "I don't know. I'm just not. Because this is a different thing. It's what I said yesterday, that we are in the position to help people for once in our lives, we can do some good, starting now. We can connect him to his wife, the love of his life."

"How do you know she's the love of his life?"

I balk. "Why else would he be doing this?"

She shrugs. "Revenge?"

I shake my head. "No way. I could feel it off him."

"His love for her?"

"His desperation."

"Doesn't mean he was in love with her."

"What are you saying?"

"I'm saying that you should probably look into it a little more. It's extremely weird, okay? I don't know if I trust this person. He wants us to open up the Veil, that's risking our lives, basically. What if his intentions aren't as pure as you think they are?"

Huh. She has a point. God, when did I stop being so jaded and cynical?

Oh yeah. The money.

"You don't know that we have to do anything with the Veil," I tell her. "He said it was Shabbadoo on Halloween, the Veil will probably be thin enough for her to walk right on through."

"Shabbadoo? Is that an Adam Sandler holiday?"

"Whatever the fuck that witchy occasion is called. I mean fuck, isn't Halloween enough? Anyway, I think it would be pretty low-risk. It's one woman, it's in a controlled environment, and for all intents and purposes, it's probably a reunion between loved ones. We're not filming a TV show out of it."

"We're not filming anything at all," she says quickly, and from the glint in her eyes, I know she was fucking reading me, since I was actually planning on bringing the camera for research purposes.

"That's not fair!" I exclaim. She's such a snoop. "Give my brain some privacy. And anyway, now it sounds like you're considering it. You're all over the place."

"Someone has to be. Anyway, I'm still thinking it over."

"You're not scared anymore?"

"I don't know. Yes. No. Maybe...maybe I don't have a reason to be. But that really all depends on their relationship, it depends on what happened to her, it depends on if this is all real or not. I mean, for all we know this might be a set-up, a prank. Maybe we'll be filmed after all, look what these losers from Experiment in Terror are doing now."

"Losers?" I say aghast, my hand on my chest. "Speak for yourself."

She leans back in her seat, staring at her hands in her lap. "I think I need to call him later."

"You think you can get a read on him that way?"

"Maybe. Worth a shot. At any rate, my instincts work pretty damn well. Gut feeling never lies."

Same went for me.

Just wish I knew what the fuck my gut was telling me now.

THREE

Thanks to the car trouble and traffic, we get to the Palomino house an hour later than usual. I have to admit, there's something nice about the suburbs this time of year, when everyone has pumpkins and jack-o-lanterns and Halloween decorations up. All we have outside our apartment is the same hobo who keeps pissing on the door.

Shit, what's happening to me? I'm actually appreciating the *suburbs*? That's where people go to give up and die.

No, it's where people go to have a family and settle down.

I don't listen to that voice. It's like it's forgotten I was born and bred in New York Fucking City.

As we slow down the street, I glance at the quaint house next to the Palomino's, which is currently occupied by one very cool couple in their sixties, Sage and Dawn Knightly.

Unfortunately there's a beige Mercedes outside, not their car.

"Fuck," I mutter, driving past it and parking the Highlander in the Palomino's driveway. "That's that freaky fucking ginger's car, isn't it?"

"Yeah," Perry says, looking past me at the vintage mobile. She looks a little troubled. "I guess Jacob's here."

Jacob "The Cobb" Edwards was the band manager for Hybrid, which was Sage Knightly's infamous rock band in the seventies. Long story short, he died decades ago when he was buried in a crypt in Prague, but apparently was pulled out of Hell, or wherever the hell he went.

Now, he's here in Portland, driving an old Mercedes.

Did I mention he's not exactly human?

Oh, and he dresses like a badly upholstered couch that wouldn't look out of place on the set of *All in the Family*. That's probably the most disturbing part of all.

"I still don't trust him," Perry says, unbuckling herself.

"Neither do I, kiddo. Neither do I."

I've only met him a handful of times when he's visiting the Knightly's. He's like Jay's mentor, the King of the Supernatural Ginger Brigade, and I guess he talks to Ada a lot too, about how to hunt demons while balancing a college education.

Thus, it shouldn't be a surprise when we grab our bags and head up the steps to the front door that it opens, displaying both Ada and Jay, her tall, immortal redwood tree of a boyfriend.

"Took you long enough," Ada says.

"I told you we had car trouble," Perry says, pulling her into a quick hug.

I give Ada a nod since she still thinks I have cooties or something, then I eye Jay. Just like Jacob, I don't trust him. He seems like he's a good match for Ada, from what I've seen, but he's one of *them*, forever a thorn in my side. Plus, there's the fact that he's like hundreds of years old or something, and Ada is technically still a teenager, even if she's now quite mature for her age.

"You going to just stand there having a pissing contest with your eyes?" Ada asks me. "Come the fuck inside."

I shake my head, realizing that I've been staring down Jay this whole time. Also just realized that he's wearing a leather jacket and white tee, like he's trying out to be a Ginger James Dean. Beats Ginger Elvis, I guess.

At that thought, a wash of sadness comes through me, but I immediately push it away. I'm good at that. It's the only way to get through.

Jay just squints at me, then lifts his giant jaw in subtle defiance and turns, heading back into the house.

Behave, Perry says, injecting her thought into my brain. She had promised not to do it too often, and she usually only does it when I'm being a dick.

I will, I tell her in my head, though I can't tell from her expression whether she's heard me or not. Probably, because she doesn't believe me either way.

We go inside. It smells comforting, like Ada's lit a bunch of scented candles called Pumpkin Spice Princess or something.

My father-in-law is standing in the kitchen with a glass of red wine filled up to the rim, the bottle next to him.

"Ah, here's the lucky couple," he says to us, and for once I don't feel his usual begrudging tolerance toward me.

"Daniel," I say to him as Perry goes over and hugs him. We aren't quite on the "dad" level yet, and our affection usually consists of a nod, sometimes even a smile. I have to admit, the man still terrifies me. He looks harmless, balding, with a pasta gut, glasses, on the short side. But I know from personal experience he has a mean right hook. Sometimes I get a phantom pain in my nose when he's around.

"Wine?" he asks us.

"Yes, always," I tell him as he grabs two glasses from the cupboard.

"Just thought I'd make sure," he says, peering at me as he uncorks the bottle of Pinot Noir. "I know it's not always recommended to drink when you're on medication."

I give him a stiff smile. Always a cheap shot somewhere.

"It's not a problem," I tell him, unable to keep the edge out of my voice.

He gives me a look I can't read and hands me my glass. "That's good to hear. I know it took you a lot of trial and error to find the right ones."

"Dad," Perry admonishes. "Why are we discussing this?"

"We're family, aren't we?" he says.

Perry's eyes dart over to Jay who is standing off to the side with Ada.

That red-headed cockwaffle is definitely *not* a part of the family.

"It's fine, Perry," I tell her. "No secrets here."

Unfortunately.

I've been on meds for about two years now. It's been a hellish process, to put it mildly, to get it just right. I know I'm no stranger to medication, and I had gone off it for a while there, which in turn opened my mind up to the super-natural again and so many other fucking things.

But the truth is, I do better on them. I've been seeing a therapist—a good one—who recently diagnosed me with ADHD. None of us were surprised in the least. I've always been ADHD personified and the writing was on the wall for years. It's just that when you've come from a fucked-up family and have gone through some pretty crazy things in your life, it's easy to blame it on other things.

So, I'm on medication for that, which has helped

immensely. So much so that I was able to be weaned off my anti-depressants (which were a total boner killer, so good riddance to that period of my life). I'm still impatient, impulsive, reckless, brash, and distracted, but at least it keeps me grounded, and in turn it's helped me become a much better husband. I hope so, anyway.

I'm also on anti-anxiety medication. The question always was whether being on meds again would affect the way I see the supernatural.

At this point, I have no idea. I haven't really seen anything since I went to Hell and back and we stopped EIT. Sure, there's been a few times where I've felt things that weren't technically there, but it's not like it used to be.

Which is yet another reason why I want to take Harry Balls up on his offer. I want to see what happens when we seek them out. I want to see if it still remains, this ability I have, or if it's been buried again.

I know Perry says she's happier pretending they don't exist.

I'm just not sure if it's the same for me.

Dealing with the dead had a way of making me feel the most alive.

"Well," Daniel says, clearing his throat and raising his wine glass. "I'm glad to see you're doing better, Dex. And even though I'm sure this is the last place you want to be for your anniversary, I have to admit I'm really grateful you're spending it with me."

Damn. Guess I do feel for the old man. I mean, I have no choice, there's nothing but emotional chaos inside him, and it's nearly impossible to keep it at a distance.

I raise my glass anyway, along with Perry, and cheers him.

"Ahem, and where's my wine?" Ada says from behind us.

"You're not twenty-one," he reminds her sternly.

"Jay is," Ada says.

I snort. Daniel gives me a funny look. I'm not about to tell him how ageless Jay really is.

"Fine," he concedes. "Would you like a glass of wine, Jay?"

I can tell from the way he talks to him that he doesn't like him anymore than I do. In fact, he might actually like me more, which says a lot.

"I better not," Jay says, glancing at Ada. "Out of solidarity."

I want to ask him if he can even get drunk anyway, but while Daniel is currently surrounded by people who experience the supernatural (including Mr. Supernatural himself), he still loves to pretend that it's all a bunch of woo woo bullshit.

"So, you're having car troubles," he says to me, changing the subject. "Toyotas are pretty reliable."

I shrug with one shoulder. "Everything has its limits. It's treated me well so far, but what I'd really like to do is trade it in and get one of the hybrids." I give Perry an expectant look.

She ignores me, smiles at her dad as she takes a sip. "The new models look like we should be driving a pack of children to a soccer game. The car will be fine."

Hmmphf.

We stand in the kitchen making small talk (her dad loves to talk about the business and then passive-aggressively drop hints that we're doing things all wrong), until Jay excuses himself, saying he has work to do next door.

I watch him leave, pausing by the door and squeezing Ada's hand before he goes.

But the moment he steps outside and starts heading next door, is the moment I realize I should be talking to Jay about our new opportunity. He might know something I don't.

"I'll be right back," I tell everyone, putting down the wine and heading out the door.

"Dex!" Ada hisses after me. "Where are you going?"

"I need to talk to your boy toy," I tell her, heading across the lawn.

"What? Why?" she cries out. "Oh god, Dex. Please don't be problematic."

I turn around, brows raised. "Problematic? *Moi?*"

Then I grin at her and run across the yard, leaping over the fence between the houses with room to spare. I manage to get right in front of Jay before he even has a chance to reach for the door.

"Do you have a moment?" I ask him.

He stares at me, then looks over at the fence that I ever-so casually jumped over like it wasn't six feet tall, then back at me again. He looks a little impressed. He should be. I'm very impressive.

"What is it?" he asks, going around me and opening the door, gesturing. "I suppose it's only polite to invite you inside."

"I'm not used to any of your kind having manners," I tell him, stepping inside the house. It's a fairly cozy place, even though it's absolutely packed with vibes, the kind that makes the hair stand up on your neck. It's not bad, per se, it's just *a lot*.

"My kind," he scoffs, shutting the door behind him. "You make me sound like an alien."

I shrug. "If the freaky shoe fits."

"Declan," a woman's voice says in surprise.

I turn to see Dawn Knightly walking down the hall toward me, a mug in her hands, steam rising out of it. I've been over here a handful of times, usually to fanboy over her husband in his jam room downstairs, but I don't dare ask her to call me Dex. She's a legend in her own right.

"What brings you here?" she asks, taking a sip of her tea and eyeing me curiously. I can tell she never really knows what to do with me.

"I was hoping to talk to Jay about something, but now that you're here too, another ear is always welcome. Where's Sage?"

"He's in the studio," she says. "I have a feeling if it's a question for the three of us, it's not going to be as simple as you borrowing a cup of sugar."

"Not exactly. I won't take up too much of your time though."

She gives me a smile that makes her look youthful against her crow's feet and gray hair. "We're retired, Declan. We have all the time in the world."

She turns and heads down the hall and I follow, the hulking redhead behind me. "Is Jacob here?" I ask, looking around. "I thought I saw his car outside earlier."

"He was, he'll be back later," she says, giving me a knowing look over her shoulder. "Something about some portal to Hell he has to go close up."

I stare. "Are you serious?"

"Hard to tell with her, isn't it?" Jay says under his breath.

While I'm still trying to figure out whether Jacob is acting as a demon bouncer or not somewhere, we walk down the stairs to the room in the basement. When the heavy door to the studio opens, sound floods out.

Sage is standing in the middle of the room, his black Les Paul hanging from his neck, some righteous tune coming from the amp.

He stops playing and looks up in surprise. "Am I being too loud?"

"Not at all," she says.

"To be honest, you could be louder," I tell him.

I know I've got the cheesiest fucking grin on my face right now. I can't help it. Not only is Sage the coolest dude I've ever met, but his jam room is amazing, and every time I'm down here I just wish everyone would leave me alone so I could geek out over all the band memorabilia and instruments without embarrassing myself.

A little background: Sage used to be in the 70's rock band Hybrid. Dawn was the young journalist sent to cover their North American tour. Jacob was their band manager, who was also managing a contract with the Devil who aimed to collect Sage before his twenty-eight birthday.

You know how it goes.

Anyway, the tour went horribly awry, people died, Dawn and Sage managed to fuck and fall in love, and now they're here, in their sixties and retired, living next door to the Palominos.

"I wasn't expecting you, Dex," Sage says, raising his hand in a high-five, and fuck yeah I never miss an opportunity to high-five a rock legend.

I slap his hand and he winces slightly, which isn't nothing when he's pretty tall and solidly built for an old dude.

"Sorry. Little too excited there." I need to calm the fuck

down. "Anyway, I just dropped by to run something past you guys."

Dawn and Sage exchange a furtive glance. "Everything okay next door?" Sage asks.

"As far as I know," Jay says, giving me an expectant look.

"It's not about them," I explain. "It's about me. And Perry."

I launch into everything about Mr. Harry Cox from beginning to end, and somehow I don't even laugh once. By the time I'm done, all three of them have completely different expressions on their faces. Sage looks wary, Dawn looks curious, and Jay, well he's impossible to get a read on. I think he just might be constipated.

"So?" I ask. "What do I do?"

"Why isn't Perry here?" Dawn asks. "Does she even know you're talking to us?"

I give her a look. "Why would you assume I'm doing this without telling her?"

Jay lets out a loud laugh.

"Shut up, Ginger," I snipe at him.

"Ginger," he says, shaking his head. "I expected a more creative insult from you, Dex."

I glare at him. "Yeah well, I ran out of all my ginger insults a long time ago." I give Dawn an apologetic smile, since she still has some fiery red in her hair. "Sorry, Dawn. You're okay."

"It's hard to say what the right thing to do is," Sage says carefully, ignoring our skirmish. "I err on the side of caution these days. I've had too many hard lessons, I'm sure you understand."

"But that's a lot of money," Dawn says to him.

"It is only if there's no catch. No exchange. Otherwise the price is too high."

Dawn turns to me. "I think if both you and Perry are open to dealing with the unknown for a night, if you think you can handle it, then it might be a great opportunity. I know why you might think there's a catch, but to me it just sounds like a man in love. Maybe I'm a romantic."

Right. Well I haven't quite told her that Perry's not really on board. I just wanted to see if these guys saw any major red flags.

Then again, Jay hasn't said anything.

I look at him. "Well?"

He folds his arms, chewing on his lip for a moment. "What are you most afraid of?"

"Clowns," I reply. "And the dentist."

He gives me a look like I'm an idiot. "I mean, what's your worst fear happening if you do this?"

"That it unleashes something. That if we contact the dead, that something else, something worse, is listening. Waiting. That we open a portal to the Veil and can't shut it. That some demon fucking beast thing comes on out. And, personally speaking, having been dragged to Hell by my brother Michael, I really don't want to go through that again."

Sage raises his hand. "Am I the only one here who hasn't died and or gone to Hell yet? Yeah? Then perhaps you better take my advice."

"You know, what you fear will harm you," Jay says to me. "If you want to do this, you have to go into it with no fear."

I laugh. "Right."

"I'm serious. And if you can avoid it, don't let Perry punch any holes into the Veil. I'm still not sure what she's capable of. I know that she can do things that Ada can't, and I'm not sure how much control she has."

"Hey, Perry's got all the control, okay? Don't you worry your pretty red head about her." I glare at him. "Anyway, if things play out like they used to with us, I'm sure we'll just roll on into that house, walk around talking to the walls, and eventually this lady will show up. That's how it worked before. You seek them out and they appear."

Although I'm a bit worried that won't be the case on my medication. At any rate, Perry will definitely see her.

"And then what?" Jay asks.

"I don't know, ask her what the weather's like over there? It's not up to me anyway, her husband is the one who wants to talk to her."

"Is he going to be there?"

"I assume so. Or maybe I'm just supposed to ask and transcribe."

Jay looks at Sage and Dawn. "Maybe I should go with them."

"Okay, just wait a fucking minute here," I tell him. "We don't need a babysitter."

"Then why did you need to talk to me about it?" he counters.

Fucker.

"I wanted your advice, that's all."

"And my advice is that I should go with you."

"Why?"

"Because I can close up the Veil if shit goes down. Because I can suss it out ahead of time and see that the coast is clear."

"Is your own babysitter going to let you do that?"

"Jacob?" Jay smirks. "Jacob doesn't have to know."

"Whoa, whoa," Dawn says, walking over to us. "Jacob

knows everything."

"Not everything," Jay says quickly, smiling about something I assume is Ada-related, but I don't want to know. "And anyway, I think it would be a good idea."

"I don't," I tell him. "We've gone the threesome route before, and it gets pretty messy."

"Tell me about it," Sage remarks.

Dawn whips around, nearly spilling her tea, and punches him on the arm. "Hey. No one needs to know about what you did with your groupies."

"*Also*," I say loudly, clearly my throat, "I was talking about being a threesome when it comes to filming. Since it's usually just us two."

"Oh he knows what you meant," Dawn says to me, rolling her eyes. "He just likes to brag about it when he can."

Sage just shrugs. Can't say I blame the man.

"So, what do you say?" Jay nods at me. "I can be the back-up, make things go smoothly. Safely."

I don't like it *at all* but that's purely because of my ego. I used to be a fucking pro at this, this was my job. Then again, the last few episodes of EIT did have either Rebecca or Maximus with us, so maybe I really do need someone else around to keep me in line. Lord knows Perry can't rein me in all the time.

"Okay. Just this once."

"Just this once?" he asks, tilting his head at me. "Is this going to be an ongoing thing."

I guess I just let that slip, didn't I?

"No," I tell him. "But maybe it'll be easier to convince Perry now that you're on board."

"You haven't convinced her yet?" Dawn practically screeches. "Declan!"

The woman sure has a way of making you feel sheepish. "What? She's stubborn. I'm just trying to, you know, stream-line things a little."

Dawn does not look impressed. Sage seems more on my side, thank god.

And Jay, well I tell Jay I'll seek him out later once I've figured out what Perry is going to say. If he can keep this from Jacob, it's worth a shot. I just don't want two supernat-ural freaks fucking with the job that Harry wants to hire me to do, especially when I trust Jacob the least.

I bid farewell to the trio and head back upstairs through the house and out the front door, just in time to see Perry marching down the driveway toward me, looking irate.

"What were you doing in there?" she asks, and from the determined look on her face, plus this dull pressure building in my sinuses, I know what she's going to try and do.

"No fair!" I yell at her, putting my hands over my ears, as if that will help. Where the fuck is a Magneto helmet when you need one?

I dodge to the left and go over the fence again, leaving her in the Knightly's yard, then run up the front steps and burst into the Palomino residence.

"Dex?" Ada says, stepping in front of me in the hall. "What's going on?"

"Tell your sister to get out of my head, please," I tell her, patting her on the shoulder as I grab my overnight bag off the floor and head up the stairs two at a time.

Okay, so I realize I'm a husband running away from his wife, but I need to compose my own thoughts first before she tries to get a read on them.

Of course Perry is stubborn as hell, so even though I'm in her old bedroom, which is now the guest room, and I've shut the door, she comes barreling in.

"You're running away from me now?" she asks, slamming the door shut.

I sit down on the bed, totally trapped. I hold up a hand in defense. "You're trying to read my mind. I had no choice."

"Because I don't know what the hell is wrong with you. You suddenly ran after Jay and disappeared into *That 70's Show*."

"I had questions."

"About the damn séance."

"Hey." I press my hands at my temples. "You said you wouldn't do that."

"I'm not trying to," she says, putting her hands on her hips. Damn it, I wish she didn't look so fucking sexy when she was yelling at me. "And even if I was, you're actually doing something to keep me out."

"Right." That's something she'd say to make me lower my guard. "So then how do you know we were talking about Harry Cox?"

"It was a lucky guess," she says, a brow quirking up. "You think I don't know you by now?" She leans in, wrapping her hands around the back of my neck, her palms warm and instantly calming me. She's got a way.

I give her a wry grin, reaching for her waist, and pulling her closer to me. "I think you know me better than I do, baby." My hands slip under her sweater, sliding against the unbearably soft skin above her jeans. I lean in slightly to kiss her, my eyes falling closed.

She pulls her head back and gives me a look.

No dice.

"Why were you talking about that with them?" she asks pointedly.

Oh right. The part where I fucked up.

"I needed a second opinion."

"And a third and a fourth?"

I shrug. "They were there."

Her hands drop away and she walks away toward the closet, staring at it for a moment, perhaps remembering all the crazy shit that went down in there a year ago. No wonder Ada wanted to change rooms again.

"You know you're a dick for not including me, right?" she says, turning around and folding her arms across her chest.

"Yes?"

"You can't just go around getting second opinions for something I haven't agreed to."

"Look, you can't blame me for being proactive."

She studies me, and I can tell she wants to snoop inside my head, but what difference does that make if she already knows me so well?

"So, what did they say?"

"Well, Dawn seemed to think it was a good idea and probably innocent. I believe she used the word romantic. Sage just wanted to talk about a threesome he had once, and Jay said he's going to be our chaperone."

"Excuse me? Our what?"

"Yeah he's volunteered to make sure we don't fuck things up. Apparently I have a history of doing that."

She wiggles her lips, which in turn makes her nose wiggle slightly, and fuck if she doesn't always look completely adorable when she does that.

Then she comes over to me and sits beside me on the bed.

"Maybe that's not a bad idea..."

I glance at her in surprise. "What, Jay coming with us?"

She nods and then puts her hand on mine. "Yeah. I'd

feel better."

"You think I can't protect you?" I have to admit, that fucking hurts.

She gives my hand a squeeze. "I worry that I can't protect *you*. I almost lost you once, Dex. I'm not going through that again. But if something like that were to happen, maybe it's good that we have one of them with us."

That hurts, too. I know I don't want Jay to be the sacrificial lamb, just like Maximus was with me. I hate how this is setting up to be that way again.

"This time will be different," she adds

"How do you know that?"

"I talked to him."

"Who?"

"Who do you think?" she says. "I called Harry while you were over there."

I break into a grin, leaning in to kiss her shoulder. "You are full of surprises, my love."

"Just trying to compete with you."

"And so...?"

She stares down at my left hand, using her forefinger to slide my wedding band around and around. "He's the real deal. Granted, I couldn't really get a read but I'm trusting my gut here and my gut says he's just a man with some money who wants one more chance to contact his wife. He says he has questions that need to be asked, even if he doesn't get the answer, and he seems to think if we do it tomorrow, we have the best shot."

"But tomorrow we're supposed to go to Cannon Beach."

"I know," she says, giving me a sweet smile. "But we can always do that after. I mean, it's our anniversary right now and we're here, so what's the difference? I'm not going anywhere."

"Neither am I," I tell her. I lean in and kiss her, slow and soft and just so fucking sweet. Her mouth opens against mine, hesitant at first, probably because she knows how I get when I kiss her like this, and that I'm two seconds away from pushing her back down on the bed and having my way with her.

Then the door springs open and Ada steps in, making us break apart.

"Jesus H. Macy," I swear. "Don't you knock?"

"You guys can make out some other time," Ada says, tucking her blonde hair behind her ear. "I'm going with you."

"What are you talking about?" Perry asks.

Ada points at the both of us. "You. Tomorrow. I'm going with you and Jay."

"How the hell did you know about that?" I ask her. "I literally just talked to him."

"While you two were about to have sex, I saw Jay," she says, sounding rightfully disgusted.

"We weren't about to have sex," Perry says, sitting up straighter, her cheeks flushing.

I give her a look. *Liar*.

"I'm going with you," Ada says with a roll of her eyes.

"I haven't even committed to going," Perry says.

"What the fuck, woman?" I stare at my wife. "You literally just did."

"Anyway, Jay approved," Ada says.

"Yes, but I don't approve," Perry says, getting to her feet. She's short, and her younger sister towers over her, and yet there's so much life force in Perry that she's completely overpowering. It's hard to explain, but it makes me very proud.

It's enough that Ada takes a step back.

"Why would you have to worry about me? Do you have any idea what I've been through over the last year?"

"I would if you opened up to me more!" Perry fires back. "You tell me nothing!"

"Ladies," I interject. "Calm your tits."

"*Dex*, please," Ada admonishes my choice of words, scrunching up her nose as she looks at me.

"Look," I tell them, splaying my palms. "If Jay says it's fine, I think it's probably fine. He knows what Ada is capable of more than we do."

"Only because she won't open to me," Perry says snidely.

Ada crosses her arms, leaning back as she appraises her sister. "Well, well, well, sounds like you can't read my mind anymore."

"I told you I wouldn't," Perry says, but from the hesitation in her eyes, I can tell she's tried.

"All I need you to know, blondie," I say to Ada, "is that the money is our money."

"What money?" she asks, eyes round.

Shit.

"We're getting paid to do this," Perry tells her reluctantly.

"How much?"

I let Perry handle that one. She gives me a nod and then shrugs at Ada. "A hundred thousand dollars."

Ada gasps. Hand at her chest. Pretends to stumble backward.

"What?! Are you serious?"

We both nod. She shakes her head. "And you only committed to this now? What the hell is wrong with you?" She stares at Perry, open-mouthed. "Do you know how much money that is?"

"I'm aware," she says carefully, running her hands down her face. She eyes the both of us. "Okay. Fine. Let's do it."

"You said that before," I remind her. "Is this for real now?"

"Yes. Let's do it."

"And I can come?" Ada asks.

"Would it matter if I said no?" Perry raises her brow.

Ada seems to think that over.

"It's going to be fine," I assure Perry. "I promise, kiddo."

"Ugh, you still call her kiddo," Ada says, walking to the door.

"Nicknames stick, Little Fifteen," I shoot back.

She leaves, sticking up her middle finger at me as she goes.

"Are you telling me I'm number one?" I call after her. If I don't get to piss Ada off at least once while I'm here, then I've failed at my duty as her brother-in-law.

"She's rude, you know," I comment to Perry, who looks pretty stressed for having just agreed to all this. "Are you okay?"

She nods. "Yeah. Yeah I just...I'm nervous. You know?"

I get off the bed and take her hands in mine. "No use being nervous about it now. We have all night tomorrow for that." I lean in and kiss her softly, pulling back to search her eyes. They carry every single color of the ocean in them. "Thank you for saying yes."

"I didn't just do it for you, Dex. I did it for us." She licks her lips, her throat moving as she swallows. "It really could change everything."

"It *will* change everything."

For better.

And hopefully not for worse.

FOUR

Dinner at the Palomino's was an interesting event, considering Daniel, once again, had no idea what was wrong with the rest of us. Perry was nervous about the whole thing and could barely eat, just pushed the food around on her plate, while Ada seemed beside herself with excitement, chatting away at a high frequency, and I was alternating between the two.

I have to say, by the time I'd gone through three large glasses of wine, trying to match Daniel, who's been drinking like a fish lately, I was leaning toward the excited side.

And I don't know if it was the wine (probably), but I was turned on as hell.

I know. I'm a fucking weirdo, and a horny bastard on my best days.

I kept thinking about what it would be like to be in that world again. The unknown. The thrill.

The fear.

Fuck, the fear got me *hard*.

So much so that I spent the end of dinner with a raging erection, trying to make the eyes at Perry so she'd get the hint and stop lingering at the table making small talk over cheesecake. It isn't until I bring my foot all the way up between her legs under the table that she finally notices me.

Her brows raise.

I give her a look. She knows the one.

She frowns, most likely because she didn't expect *that* look at the dinner table.

"Need any help cleaning up?" she asks her father, getting out of her chair.

Oh god, I am in no position to do the dishes, why is she volunteering us?

But Daniel just waves her away. "I've got it. Ada will help."

Ada shoots Perry a dirty look but it's too late, Perry is heading to the stairs and I'm pushing my chair back while thanking Daniel for dinner, and then I'm hot on her trail.

We're down the hall, near the bedroom, when she turns around and eyes me suspiciously. "Are you drunk? What's wrong with you?"

The question should be, what's right with me?

Right now? Everything.

I don't say that though.

Instead, I usher her inside the room, close the door, locking it shut, and then I'm on her.

She lets out a little yelp of surprise as I grab her face in my hands, kissing her deeply, walking her backward until her legs hit the end of the bed. Her hands go up to the neck of my t-shirt and she grips it, holding me back as she pulls away.

"Dex," she says, trying to find her breath, her eyes searching mine. "What happened?"

"Everything," I tell her, managing a smirk before the hunger overwhelms me. It starts as a building fire in the base of my balls, igniting up my spine until my mouth is on hers again, fucking her with my tongue, driven by some strangely insatiable need. If she's caught off-guard, so am I, but like hell if I'm going to do a thing to stop it.

She moans into my mouth, and Christ on a cracker, that sets me off like nothing else.

My hands work feverishly all over her body, pulling up at her sweater, tugging down at her jeans, feeling acute desperation, like if I didn't stick my dick inside her and come right here, right now, I might possibly die. A tragic death by blue balls.

Thankfully Perry gets over her confusion and hesitation at me mauling the fuck out of her and reads into my urgency. She unzips her jeans and tries to step out of them, but I impatiently shove her back onto the bed.

"I'm going to fuck the hell out of you," I practically growl at her, pulling my shirt over my head, taking off my pants. I slip off my boxer briefs, my cock standing at attention, painfully hard.

Perry's eyes go round and, sweet Jesus, the fact that my dick still gets that reaction from her is priceless.

"Spread your legs," I tell her, making a fist over my cock and sliding it slowly up my shaft. I have to be careful as fuck or I'm going to jack myself off with ease.

Her cheeks go pink, and that only turns me on even more. My god, I'm just torturing myself right now.

"You're bossy tonight," she says, biting her lip. "I like it. Just tell me what to do."

A rush runs through me, and holy hell am I the luckiest fucker alive.

"Get yourself off," I tell her. "Let me watch."

Whenever we fuck, I almost always make Perry come twice. That's the bare minimum. The only problem now is,

I am so damn horny that if I go down on her right now, I'm going to end up coming into the bedspread like I'm fourteen years old again. The taste of her alone can set me off on my good days.

So yeah, this time I'm going to let her get herself off so I can fuck her hard and fast and be done with this painful, primal surge that's threatening to pull me apart.

She moves into it fast, too. Her legs spread wider, showcasing the glistening pink of her cunt, her fingers working herself. She's surprisingly uninhibited, considering she usually keeps a part of her guarded, even during sex, even after all this time. But I guess whatever I'm feeling right now, that buzzing in my veins, the pounding in my chest like I've just been injected with steroids, she's feeling it too.

I watch her closely, in awe, as her back arches and her perfect creamy tits rise, her tight little nipples pointing at the ceiling. Her mouth is open, eyes pinched shut in concentration, and I am fucking dumbstruck by two competing feelings that are starting to merge into one: how much I love this woman, and how much I want to fuck her brains out.

My dick is a monster and I have to grip it hard, force myself to think of bad memories in order to have some modicum of control, especially as I watch her come to a climax, the tiny, breathless cries that spill from her open lips, the way she's writhing on the bed.

Thinking unsexy thoughts isn't going to get me anywhere. If I keep this up, I'm going to come while imagining something awful, and that wouldn't be fun.

She's still convulsing when I get on the bed and prowl over her, moving fast, feeling like time is running out. I steady myself between her legs and she looks up at me with big, sated eyes as I push myself inside her with one hard, slick thrust.

We both cry out, the air expelled from our lungs, and my eyes practically roll to the back of my brain. I'm buried in so deep, I swear I'm being fused to her.

But this was always the case with her.

Our connection is like no other.

And when I'm inside her, when I'm moving in her body, when we're tangled together as one, it's like we're two magnets unable to keep apart. This isn't just about the sex, about the nearly supernatural desire and pleasure that we give each other, this is about our souls. This is where they meet, meld, lock together.

But fuck it if I'm not a slave to this need to get off right now.

"Dex," she says through a moan, her hands going into my hair, making tiny fists, trying to hold on even though I can't be stopped, not now, not when I'm losing my fucking mind to her body.

I'm rutting into her, raw and ruthless, my ass cheeks clenching with unlimited power as I drive into her, again and again, deeper and deeper. She makes these incredible noises that are nothing short of a symphony and I'm the conductor.

"Jesus," she swears, hands going down my back now in an effort to contain me as I thrust harder, faster. I bury my head into her neck, biting her there until I taste blood.

She gasps in pain.

Sweat pours off me.

The bed slams against the wall.

The smell of sex fills the room.

"Dex, Dex, oh god," she cries out, clawing at my back in

vicious scratches, and I can't hold it together any longer. I feel her clench around me as the breath inside her stills.

Then she's unleashed, quaking beneath me.

And I come so motherfucking hard it feels like I've been hit by a truck.

"Fuck!" I call out, my mind going black and blank, the roar of the orgasm ripping me apart at the seams. "Holy fucking FUCK."

I'm blabbering now, barely aware that my thrusts are slowing down, that I'm still coming inside her somehow, like there's a dam inside me that won't subside.

But eventually it does.

I collapse on top of her, trying to get air back into my lungs, my heart thundering against my ribs so hard I feel like it's trying to meet hers.

What the hell just happened there?

We have sex a lot. Sometimes it's freaky.

But it's been a long time since it's been like that.

I don't even have words for it.

"Dex," Perry says softly.

I lift up my head and gaze at her, my eyes trying to focus.

My god, she's beautiful.

And to think she's mine.

"I'm sorry, am I crushing you?" I ask, licking my lips, making a sorry attempt to push off of her.

"No!" she cries out, eyes flashing. She grabs my shoulders, holding me against her chest, the sweat of my exertion sticking between us. "No. Don't. I just..."

"I know," I manage to say, smoothing her hair off her forehead. I eye the bitemark on her neck. I hate that it turns me on, like I've left my permanent mark there. I guess a wedding band isn't enough. "I got carried away."

She nods slowly, her eyes resting on my mouth, my nose, searching the corners of my face, like she can't really believe it's me. "I didn't mind," she says softly. She swallows, nostrils flaring. "I can't remember the last time I came that hard."

I give her a wry smile. "Gee, thanks."

"I can't remember the last time you came like that either," she says. "Something changed."

"Nothing changed," I tell her quickly.

But, of course something has.

It's what we're about to do tomorrow.

It's that step into the past.

Into the unknown.

Into the fear.

And if I wasn't afraid of spooking her, I'd probably tell her my theory.

That sex heals me, it's a balm on the wounds I bury deep.

It quiets the chaos of my mind.

And it strengthens that bond between us when we're going to need it most.

"Well, that was one hell of an anniversary present," she says, as if that was to blame.

And then I realize fuck, I never bought her an anniversary gift. I thought that having a romantic night somewhere would be enough, but of course that's not enough, you always get the wife something else nice as an extra. And now we're not even going to the beach at all. Instead we're going to be re-enacting scenes from *Beetlejuice* with her sister and the Cheeto-head.

Dex, you fucking tool. Worst husband of the year award, right here.

Oh well. At least there was the orgasm.

I pull out and roll off of her, also aware that the chances of her sister and father hearing us were quite high.

I think from the way she's sitting up, looking sheepish, she's thinking the same thing.

"If anyone asks, we'll just tell them we had to battle the closet monsters again," I tell her, slipping on my briefs. I toss her her bra and sweater.

"Dex, don't talk about that," she warns me, eyes darting to the closet.

"Hey, that's all done with. You know that."

But for how long? Her voice whispers softly in my head.

I guess we'll see.

~

THE NEXT DAY ROLLS AROUND IN HARMONY WITH Halloween. The morning is foggy and dark gray, with trails of mist moving through the fir trees outside the window in the kitchen.

I'm sitting at the table, mainlining coffee, along with Ada and Perry.

The two of them are quiet as they pick at their breakfast, then they occasionally look at each other in either surprise or annoyance, which makes me think they might be having a conversation in their heads. Either way, I'm not about to get involved in their sisterly business, which seems more and more complicated by the day. Judging by the way Perry is keeping her hair wrapped around the bite mark I left on her, Ada is probably giving her shit about that.

Honestly, I'm in my own world, trapped in my own head. My thoughts are bouncing back and forth on a loop, as it happens sometimes. I have good days and bad days, and some days the medication isn't enough, I need extra coffee to power through. Or a cigarette. Fuck, I would kill for a cigarette.

I keep thinking about two things.

One is the sex I had last night, because I'm nothing if not on-brand.

And two is what we're about to do tonight.

As for the sex, I'm not sure what exactly came over me, but I have a feeling that it won't be a one-time thing. There's something in my blood that runs hot, saturating my veins like smoke, that pulls at me. Pulls me back to those same feelings from last night. The lust. The insatiable wild necessity. Like some primal, lizard-brained part of me is waking up for the first time in a long time and it only has one need.

And that's to fuck.

It's not some vague feeling either. It's specific in its want.

It's focus is solely for the woman sitting across from me, biting into a piece of toast, her eyes going to the window and taking in the rolling fingers of fog.

That's who I want.

More than anything.

And I know I have her...I know I do. That's the funny thing about all of this. Perry is mine and always will be. She's wearing a ruby and topaz ring on her left hand, the ring I gave her. The ring that symbolizes our marriage, just as the band on my finger does.

So she's mine, I know she's mine.

Then why do I feel...I *need* to keep her?

With a desperation I hadn't felt in years?

And why does this desperation make me feel so fucking alive?

Which brings my brain back to the other thing I'm obsessing over.

Tonight.

The reason why I have goosebumps all over my body already.

Why the hair on the back of my neck is already raised, like whatever we're about to do has already started, just by our own intentions.

Plus, I have a hard-on.

I'm a fucking mess of a man.

"Are you okay?" Ada asks me.

I glance over at her, wondering what she's picking up on.

I give her a quick smile, adjusting myself. "I'm fine."

She studies me, suspicious as always, then has a sip of her coffee before glancing at Perry.

Perry is still staring out the window, oblivious to either me or Ada.

"Then stop looking at her like that," Ada says.

My brows raise. "*Pardon?* Stop looking at my wife?"

"Yeah. It's weird. You're looking at her like she's food."

"*Food?*" I pause. "What kind of food?"

Ada rolls her eyes. "Look, I just want things to go smoothly tonight, and it's quite obvious that you're just rolling with your feelings right now."

"I'm not *rolling* with anything," I counter. "I'm just... getting prepared."

Don't tell me she can hear thoughts too now.

But while I'm talking with Ada, I notice Perry hasn't said a word. She's still staring out the window.

"Perry?" I say softly, trying to not look at her like a fucking Big Mac or whatever the fuck food Ada was talking about.

She still doesn't look at me.

Finally I reach across the table and take her hand.

She blinks, jolted back into reality and looks at me in surprise.

"God. Sorry, I..." She shakes her head and looks at the both of us. "I was daydreaming. There are these birds out there. They're so strange..."

I follow Perry's gaze out the window, across the lawn to the towering maple trees on the other side of the road. I don't know how I didn't notice it before, considering the branches are mostly bare, with a few patches of orange leaves hanging on, but there's a giant flock of tiny birds that keep taking off and landing on the trees.

The birds take off as one, like a black cape, swirling and twirling up into the air and then swoop back down, covering the trees. They stay there for a moment, chirping and bouncing along the branches, before they do it again. A blot in the sky.

Leave as one.

Land as one.

A chill runs down my spine.

I twist in my seat to look at Ada and Perry.

Perry's expression is blank, almost dreamy. Ada looks bothered.

"I hope that's not an omen," Ada says.

"I wonder what they're doing," Perry muses softly.

"Oh good, you're still here," Daniel says, walking into the kitchen with a newspaper under his arm, maybe the only person alive who still reads them. He breaks up the weird vibes, with all of us snapping to attention.

He puts the newspaper down and stares at us, like he has something to say.

Then he looks at me.

I can't read his expression, but I can feel what he's carrying in him.

Worry and fear.

But he doesn't know what we're up to tonight, unless Ada has told him.

"Dex," he says, grabbing the coffee pot and pouring himself a cup. "You're good at gardening, right?"

Perry snorts. "Dad, have you met Dex?"

But what Perry isn't picking up on, what she *should* be picking up on, is that the conversation is a ruse.

"I know some things," I tell him, and god help me if I'm wrong about this because I know shit-all. I've had numerous marijuana plants over the years, and they've all died. Probably because I didn't water them. Look, I can barely take care of myself.

"Perhaps you can tell me what's wrong with the fig tree in the back yard," he says, walking across the kitchen with his cup of coffee, gesturing with his head to the sliding doors in the living room.

"Uh, yeah, I can do that," I say, avoiding the rapid-fire looks that Ada and Perry are shooting me.

I get up and follow Daniel, my palms sweating.

I feel like I'm in trouble.

Like I've done something wrong.

He's about to go all Italian mafia on my ass, isn't he?

I'm out of the family, just like that.

We step through the doors and onto the patio, the floor cold and damp through my socks. He slides the door closed behind us.

What are you doing? Perry comes into my head, but I just shut my eyes for a moment, booting her back out.

"You okay, Dex?" Daniel asks.

I look at him, giving him a quick smile. "Oh fine. Just a bit concerned you might be plotting to murder me and have a quick burial."

I expected him to laugh at that, or at least smile, but he doesn't do either.

"Here's the thing," he says. "This isn't about the fig tree."

"You mean that fig tree?" I ask, pointing to a small one in a large white pot.

He glances over his shoulder at it. "Yes."

"Well I can tell you one thing, you need to plant it soon. It won't do too well in a pot."

He frowns at me. "So you do know how to garden?"

Honestly, I'm just making shit up. I shrug. "So, what is this about, if not about figs?"

He sighs and pinches the bridge of his nose before adjusting his glasses. "Okay. You have to promise me you won't tell Ada or Perry about this."

Oh no. I'm being sworn to secrecy. That's not the easiest thing around my wife.

I swallow. "You know, I'm not the best with secrets."

"Then you'll have to try, alright?" He says sternly.

"Yes, sir."

"I've been having...visions."

"Visions? Like...of the Virgin Mary?"

"No," he says sharply. "You know I'm not a priest, right? Anyway."

"Right, right. The visions."

"You're going to think I'm crazy, but I keep seeing Ingrid."

My heart goes still. Perry's mother.

"That's not a crazy thing," I try to reassure him. "That's normal."

"It's not normal," he says, a wild spark in his eyes. He's shaking his head. "She keeps telling me the same thing over and over again. Like she's stuck on repeat. I see her before I go to bed at night. I see her in the morning. Sometimes I see her in the middle of the road. Sometimes the mirror. It should be comforting Dex, but it's not."

The chills are back, cascading down my spine. Above us, in the misty sky, a flock of birds flies past, chattering and moving as one until they disappear.

I swallow thickly, the cold in the air seeping to my bones. "What, uh, what does she keep saying?"

He stares at nothing for a moment, and even though I'm trying not to pick up on anything, I know he's waging a war with himself. That he thinks he's crazy.

"You're not crazy," I quickly tell him. "Let's just settle that right now. And these aren't just tricks of your mind either. You know by now, you've seen enough."

He grimaces, then nods sharply in agreement. "You're right. It's not my mind. But I have to pretend it is, don't you see? Or I really will lose it. I can't afford that. I'm all my daughters have left."

"What is Ingrid saying?" I ask again.

"She keeps saying...don't let her."

"Don't let her what?"

"That's just it. I don't know. I've asked. I ask and I ask and that's all she says. She pleads. Don't let her, don't let her."

More chills, the rawness in my father-in-law's voice.

"And you don't know who she's talking about...Perry or Ada?"

He shakes his head. "No," he says quietly, staring at the ground. Then he glances up at me. "That's why I told you, Dex. Because I know, no matter who she's talking about, you'll be there to protect her. Protect the both of them when you can."

"I think Jay can look out for Ada," I tell him. I hate to

stick up for him, but I at least believe he protects her and cares for her.

"Nah," he says dismissively. "I don't like him."

"Neither do I, but...your daughter has been dating him for a year."

"She says they aren't dating," he says. "If you can believe it."

I smile. "Not as tricky as she thinks." I pause, my stomach starting to feel unsettled. "Do you have any idea at all what your wife would have meant?"

"I really don't."

"And you think it's her?"

Not, like a demon, I finish in my head.

"I don't know what I think, Dex."

"And you don't want to tell them?"

"I don't want to worry them. Talking about their mother...it's hard. I know neither of them are okay yet. I know I'm not. I'm not sure when I will be either. I just...I want to keep them safe and in the dark, for as long as I can, until I can figure out what's going on. But in the meantime... just look out for them, Dex. Look out for Perry. I'll watch Ada as closely as I can, but only you can protect Perry." He rubs his lips together, making a face. "I know you have so far."

"Was that so hard to say?" I ask, half-joking.

He puts his hand on my shoulder. "You love her. I know you do. Just keep loving her, please."

Good lord. His words are breaking my heart.

"I love her more each morning than I did when I went to sleep."

"Good," he says after a moment. "And hopefully this is just me worrying for nothing. I have been stressed lately, drinking a little too much. Perhaps it's a wake-up call to stop the booze. Maybe the hallucinations will go away."

But I know that's not the case.

It takes a lot to get a man like Daniel Palomino to admit he's seeing ghosts.

Unfortunately, whatever message Ingrid is passing on is an important one.

Too bad we don't know what it means.

FIVE

"So he doesn't trust Jay?" Perry asks.

We've been driving for about an hour, and she's been grilling me non-stop on the whole exchange with her father. Naturally, I had to cover the truth with a lie, one that she'd believe.

"No, he doesn't," I tell her for the millionth time. Not a lie either.

"No wonder he seemed so bothered by them coming to Seattle for the night. Wait, you didn't tell him anything about the haunted house, did you?"

I give her a loaded glance. "Come on."

"Okay, just checking."

After Daniel dumped that secret on me, which I really want to chalk up to him just having too much to drink and hallucinating, the rest of us got going. Perry and I in our car, Jay and Ada smushed together in her Mini Cooper, which she just raced past us on the I-5 only moments ago.

Of course, Ingrid's words are bouncing around in my head now.

Don't let her. Don't let her.

Who? What?

If it's Perry, what isn't she supposed to do?

Buy the overpriced Slayer vinyl she's been eying on Ebay?

Or, like, go into this haunted house tonight?

Or is it something much deeper than that?

And if it's Ada, same questions apply.

There's just not enough to go on, and it's not like I can stop Perry from doing anything in the first place.

You just need to protect her, I remind myself. Love her, fuck her, protect her. That's always been my duty.

"So why did he talk to you about her and not me?" she asks, snapping me out of it.

I sigh tiredly and go back to lying. "Because he didn't want you to worry about her. You already worry about her enough. I guess he wanted me to look out for her, you know, since I'm a big tough man and all that." When she doesn't say anything, I glance at her. "Don't you dare laugh."

She presses her lips together, eyes dancing. "I'm not laughing because I know you're stronger than anyone has a right to be. But my dad doesn't know that."

"Look, just because he got a good punch at me once..."

Truth be told, I like that people underestimate me. They think because I'm not over six feet, and that I'm not crazy bulky, that I can't possibly possess the strength that I do. But I do. And my favorite thing is catching people completely off-guard.

Not that I ever want to challenge her father to a boxing match or anything.

Not really.

When we finally get back to downtown Seattle, it's just us two. Ada and Jay went to Target for some reason, and while I'm usually pretty lenient, I put my foot down when

Perry said she wanted to join them. That place is worse than Wal-Mart. At least in Wal-Mart, you're in and out, lest you get sucked in and become of those Wal-Mart people you see on the internet. Target is the same pig in a different shade of lipstick, and I have no idea how it captures women for hours, how they disappear inside the cavernous white walls looking for toothpaste and a bag of Cheetos and yet come out with five-hundred-dollars worth of crap, all disoriented, not remembering why they even went in there in the first place.

Did I mention how much I hate Target?

So we get back to an empty apartment. Fat Rabbit has been with our friends, Dean and Rebecca, since we thought we'd be celebrating at a fancy hotel tonight instead of going ghost-hunting.

Ghost-hunting.

I never thought those words would cross my mind again, and yet they are.

That's what we're doing tonight.

Call it a séance, call us mediums, call us two amateurs trying to talk to the dead.

But we're hunting for ghosts.

Fuck-a-doodle-do.

This shouldn't feel this good.

Ah...

And there it is again.

This strange electricity in the air between us as Perry walks in and throws her bag down on the sofa, her posture immediately relaxing now that she's home. She pauses, her back to me, raising her arms above her head in a long satisfying stretch.

I can't help myself. I walk over to her, my veins buzzing like I've just been plugged into a socket. Those raw, desperate feelings I felt earlier are back with a vengeance.

I put my hand at the back of her neck, grabbing her there, and pull her around to me. She lets out a gasp, spinning on her feet, and I bring her crashing against my mouth, kissing her hard and hungry.

She kisses me back, fueling the fire, my hands drift to her jeans, trying to unbuckle them, my fingers fumbling, not working fast enough.

But then her palms are on my chest, pushing me back.

We break apart.

I stare at her, feeling fucking crazy and wild, breathing hard.

She stares back at me in complete confusion.

"What has got into you?" she says, her eyes huge. "*Dex.*" She presses her fingers into my chest, as if she's checking to make sure it's me.

And it *is* me.

I've never felt more like myself.

"We're alone," I tell her, my voice going husky. Do I have to actually tell her that I just want to screw her like crazy right now, right here in the living room?

"Not for long," she says. "Ada and Jay had a head start, they'll be here any second." She licks her lips, blinking. "Look, last night was amazing but..."

"But what?" I ask quickly.

Oh god, is that...rejection that I'm starting to feel?

Is this her payback for not letting us go to Target?

"I'm just not used to this," she says carefully.

"Not used to this?" I repeat. "We used to fuck non-stop."

"Yes, we did," she says, her cheeks flushing, and fuck, of course that also turns me on. I couldn't be harder, even when she's turning me down. "We did. Back then. And then we got married and it slowed down and that was okay too."

She's leaving out the period when I was on anti-depressants where it didn't just slow down, it completely stopped. We survived that lurch, but it wasn't a lot of fun. Sure, my brain felt better, but when your dick doesn't cooperate, and you can't fuck your wife on the regular, it does wear on you. Our connection suffered.

Then again, I went down on her all the time, so I'm not sure she faired as badly as I did.

"What are you saying?"

"I'm saying I...I don't know what's come over you, but something has. And it's not that I don't like it, I do. I'm just...a little caught off-guard."

I place my hands on her face and hold her in place, running my thumb over her bottom lip. "Baby, I don't know what it is, but lately, I've been feeling so damn alive. I can't help it. Like all I want to do is feel alive with you. And part of feeling this alive is getting you completely naked and fucking you six ways from Sunday."

She swallows, nodding, her eyes searching mine, looking sweet. "Lately? Or just the last twenty-four hours?"

Okay, she has me there.

"Dex," she says patiently. "I know you like I know the back of my hand. I've watched you through these years. I know how you were when we were doing the show, I know how you were after. You have always been easily excitable, even on medication, but I haven't felt...*this*," she gestures with her hand at me in a circle, "I haven't felt this in a long time. And I know it's less about the money now, less about the excitement of how that will change our lives, and more about fucking around with the dead. In fact, if Harry called and told you he wouldn't be able to pay us tonight as planned, you'd probably still want to do it for free. Wouldn't you?"

I don't have to say anything. She knows.

"And that's fine," she goes on. "I get it. I know you. I wouldn't expect anything less. But it's all connected."

"Are you saying that dealing with the supernatural, or just the thought of it, is turning me into raging horndog?"

She laughs, her eyes crinkling at the corners. Such a beautiful face.

"Yes. That's exactly what I'm saying. I feel like I'm dealing with the old you. And that's not a bad thing, but that's what's happening. You've got so much fucking adrenaline in your system that it has nowhere else to go."

I know Perry is right about all of that, but I also know that it goes a few layers deeper too. It was what I was thinking last night. That this is about establishing a connection between us before we need it the most.

I just refuse to let myself think about *why* we need it the most.

"And look," she goes on, wrapping her hands around my neck and staring up at me, "I don't want you to think you can't have me when you want me. You can. Believe me, I'm…well, let's just say I welcome it. Part of me is feeling this too. But I just need a little time to adjust. So until then, just keep it in your pants, okay?"

She gives me a teasing smile and then reaches down, pressing her palm against my erection, eliciting a groan from my mouth.

"That's not fair." I practically whimper, grinding against her hand. "You play a dirty game, Perry Foray."

The apartment buzzer goes off.

She looks at me triumphantly. "Told you they'd be here."

She gives me one last hard squeeze and then heads over to the buzzer.

She's right, but that doesn't mean my hard-on is disappearing anytime soon.

That is, until she opens the door and Ada and Jay walk in. One look at that wankhammer and I completely deflate.

"Surprise!" Ada calls out, lifting Target shopping bags high in the air.

"What now?" I grumble.

She looks up at Jay with a mischievous smile, but I swear the big redhead looks pained. "I got us Halloween costumes!"

"You did what?"

"It's Halloween, you guys," she says, looking at us like we're totally out of touch. "And so, I got us costumes. Obviously."

I cross my arms, feeling mildly amused. "Ada, what do you think is going to happen tonight? This isn't a Halloween party. We're not going trick-or-treating."

"It doesn't matter," she says, plopping the bags on the counter and rummaging through them. "You guys are in such weird moods, I thought I would lighten things up. This can be fun, you know."

"We're not in weird moods," Perry protests.

Ada glances at her through her blonde hair that's fallen over her eyes. "Uh huh. You keep telling yourselves that." She jerks a thumb at me. "This guy over here, well, let's just say I'm glad I can't hear what he's thinking." Her eyes go to Perry. "And you, well you're putting up your tough front, but I know how scared you are about doing this."

Don't let her, don't let her.

I close my eyes, trying to bury those words, almost as if I'm hearing Ingrid say them herself.

"Dex?" Jay asks.

My eyes pop open to see him staring at me, brow furrowed.

"Yes, what?" I say, trying to play it off.

Except, shit. What if what Ingrid was telling Daniel really was about tonight?

Oh god, I've never done well with conflicting feelings.

On one hand, we need the money, and I want, need, this to happen.

On the other hand, maybe it's a bad idea.

Maybe it's a *really* bad idea.

I clear my throat. Everyone is already looking at me. "Jay," I say to him. "Since we're all here talking, relatively safe, haven't fully committed to anything we can't back out of...I'm going to need some supernatural reassurance from you."

His brow raises. "What do you mean?"

"Ever since I told you about this...have you had any pushback? Any bad feelings? Any voices from the other side telling you that it's a bad idea?"

He shakes his head. "No."

That should make me feel better, but...

"You still haven't told Jacob," I point out.

"He hasn't been around," he says, eyes narrowing for a moment.

"But would you if he hadn't gone off to close some demon portal?"

"He's doing what now?" Perry interjects.

Jay ignores her. Wiggles his jaw. "No."

"Why not?"

"Because he gets too involved," Ada says quickly. "Now don't tell me you're having second thoughts."

I raise my hands. "I wouldn't be a very good man if I didn't. I just want to make sure that we're all one hundred percent on board and that none of us have any doubts. Or warnings that you've brushed off. Each and every one of us are tapped into something bigger than us, the unknown, the Veil. Whatever you want to call it. We each have some sort of ability or, fuck, affliction, when it comes to dealing with the dead. Obviously some of us here aren't even mortal or human. I won't mention names. But I think if we're going to be successful tonight, and safe, we all need to be honest."

I know I'm the one not being honest. That I'm carrying Daniel's secret with me. But since I don't know what the hell Ingrid meant, then I can't say it has anything to do with tonight. If it did, I'm more than certain one of these three would have felt something.

Right?

"Well, I think the whole thing will be fun," Ada says. "I don't have any gut feelings telling me this is wrong or dangerous or something."

Hmmm. That doesn't really help. Ada would be the type to have gone to Hell and come back thinking it was a fun trip.

I look at Jay.

He shrugs. "I don't have any issues with this. I'm here just in case, but it sounds pretty straightforward to me. Go in the house, try to summon his wife, ask her some questions, and leave. You don't need to open up the Veil. In fact, to make things even more simple, if you can't contact her, just leave it at that. You don't have to go looking for trouble."

I know I find Jay sketchy sometimes, and that's due to

the nature of what he is and my own personal experiences with "Jacobs," but I believe what he says.

Finally I look at Perry. "And you, kiddo?"

She gives me a wan smile. "You know how I feel. I'm scared. That hasn't changed. But I think there's a part of me that's excited too. More than that, I'm focused on what the money can bring us. It makes handling these fears worth it."

"So you're not scared enough to put up your hand and tell me no?"

"Dex, you know I will if it comes to it."

That I know. I've had more than enough experience putting Perry in risky and dangerous situations where she's put up her hand and told me it was too much.

Unfortunately, there've been a few occasions where I've ignored that and pushed her anyway. I'd like to think I've grown out of that.

"Okay then," Ada says, clapping her hands together. "Then it's settled. We're going, and we're going to have some fun while we're at it. Dex, you're first."

"First with what?"

She grins, pulling out a few tubes of face makeup and a sponge, coming at me like a serial killer. "Your costume."

A COUPLE OF HOURS LATER, THE FOUR OF US ARE sitting in the fireside lounge at the Sorrento Hotel in the First Hill neighborhood, drinking beer and mulled wine, all of us in costume (along with everyone else in this place).

Ada decided to go the sexy Mother of Dragons route from *Game of Thrones*, her hair braided and little dragons stuck all over her, while Jay got off easy and is just wearing a kilt. He's supposed to be some character from *Outlander*, and with his stupid chiseled face he probably fits the role well.

Perry doesn't look that different from normal. Her long black hair is in soft waves, she's wearing red lipstick that shows off the shape of her plump perfect lips. But she's poured herself into a long black velvet gown that is way too tight for her breasts and they're spilling over like they're trying to escape their velvet prison.

She's Morticia Addams.

My teenage crush. I don't even want to think about all the hours I spent jacking off to Angelica Houston in those movies.

I feel like Ada knew I'd lose my mind over this, hence why she got it for Perry, and she was right. I am going fucking mental, peeling back the labels on my beer bottle like I've got SEXUALLY FRUSTRATED written all over my face.

Then there's me.

Naturally, I'm Gomez Addams.

Not that I'm particularly complaining. Though I've been wearing more of a beard lately, I shaved it off and left the mustache. Ada darkened it with black paint, put white makeup on the rest of my face, then ringed my eyes with dark liner. I slicked my hair off my face with a fuckload of gel, and put on a ridiculously ill-fitting striped suit that smells like plastic, and then the bowtie.

I have to say, I look the part.

And just like Gomez continuously lusted after his wife, I'm doing the same to mine.

But Perry's mind is elsewhere again, and even though the restroom is right around the corner, and I would be very, *very* quick with her, she did tell me to keep it in my pants. So I sit back, drink my beer, and take it out on the label.

The reason we're at this hotel is because it's in the neighborhood of Harry Cox's house (not even snickering at his name anymore). First Hill is directly east of downtown, and one of the oldest residential areas of the city. The buildings and religious institutions here are vibing with energy, and the address he gave us is about a ten-minute walk from here. Plus, a few pre-ghost-hunting cocktails will probably help with the nerves.

Jay looks around at the wood-paneled walls of the lounge. "You know this place is haunted, right?"

"What?" Perry and I both say in unison, our heads swiveling toward him.

He gives us a curious look. "I thought you would have both picked up on that. The Veil is very thin here. There are things I'm seeing that you're obviously not."

I glance at Perry and she shrugs. "I'm not seeing anything unusual," she says, her eyes scanning the crowd. "Though everyone is in costume so that doesn't help. I mean that guy over there is dressed as a tub of Mayonnaise."

"I don't see anything either," Ada says. "Oh wait, what about that vampire in the corner over there?"

Jay looks over his shoulder at the vampire trying to sip a cocktail with his fangs and laughs. "Not a ghost."

For a moment I thought my ability was hampered by the medication, but if every normal person couldn't see them, then it wasn't just me.

"Maybe we're all a little rusty," I tell him, glancing at the grandfather clock by the fireplace. "And maybe we should get going. Doesn't hurt to be early."

"You, on time for something?" Perry asks incredulously, finishing her drink. "I don't believe it."

I get to my feet and hold out my hand. "Believe it, *Cara Mia*," I say in my best Gomez impression.

I can tell by the way her cheeks go pink that she likes this as much as I do. I don't know how I could be attractive with this particular mustache, and the eye makeup, but I guess it does something for her.

But my plans for ravishing her will have to wait until we get home, whether that's tonight or in the early morning hours.

"You know," Jay says to me as we leave the hotel, stepping out into the foggy, cold night. Firecrackers go off in the distance, the air smelling acidic. "If you ever do think about starting up your show again, that hotel would be a great place to start."

"That ain't happening," Perry says, giving Jay a sharp look. "There's a reason why we're not filming this. Tonight is about the money, not a step backward."

"Tell me how you really feel," I say under my breath.

"*Dex*," she says, pulling at my arm, eyes flashing. "Please tell me that this is just a one-time thing. Unless someone else wants to pay us an obscene amount of money, we're not doing this again. We have to agree on that."

"Yeah, yeah," I tell her, but I can tell from the way Jay's looking at me that he's thinking about what I said yesterday. He only had to help *just this once.*

I ignore him and try to keep my thoughts focused on tonight, not the future, not where this might take us, as tempting as that might be.

We walk down the dark street, fallen leaves crunching beneath our feet. There are still a few groups of trick-or-treaters straggling about, but most of them are idle drunk teenagers trying to make the night last. It's nearly ten p.m., only two more hours until the supposed witch holiday comes to an end.

"This should be the house, right on the corner," I say,

staring at the GPS on my phone. We come to a stop and stare.

The house is haunted as fuck.

I don't have to see anything spooky to know it, and judging from the chill in the air, the silence that thickens between the four of us, we're all feeling it.

The house is three-stories tall, the bottom half brick, the rest timbered. In the dim light of the flickering streetlight, it looks sick in color, this yellowish beige, framed with dark brown. The windows on the first two levels are all boarded up and the house looks completely dark, save for a faint light coming from one of the windows on the third floor.

There's a set of stairs leading to the door, which, in the dark, looks almost like a church door, angled at the top.

Yeah, this is some scary fucking shit already and we're still standing on the street, holding our breath as if the house is about to take it from us.

Maybe this isn't a good idea?

SIX

I CAN'T TAKE MY EYES OFF THE HOUSE.

It's like it's been...*waiting* for us.

"Hello!" A man suddenly darts in front of us, and the four of us scream and jump in unison.

"Holy shit," Ada yells, hand to her chest.

"I'm so sorry," the man quickly says, holding his palms out at us. "I was sent here to you meet you."

I try to control my heart, which is bouncing around against my ribs, focusing on the man. It's hard to see him clearly in the dark. He's about six feet tall, dark wavy hair, light eyes, bit of a tan, my age, maybe a bit younger or older, it's hard to tell. He's wearing a black trench coat, which probably accounts for us not seeing him until he was right in front of us.

I can't get a read on him either. His vibes are a bit...off. Foggy, like the mist around us.

"You must be Dex and Perry," the man says to us, then squints at Ada and Jay. "I'm sorry, I don't know who you are."

"Actually, we don't know who *you* are," I tell him.

"Right," he says. "I'm Atlas. Atlas Poe."

"Atlas Poe?" I repeat, snorting. "As if that's your real name."

"I'm afraid it is. But it could be worse. I could have my stepfather's name. Harry Cox?"

"Harry is your stepfather?" Perry asks him. "He never mentioned you."

"I suppose he wouldn't," he says with a tired sigh. "He's very singularly focused these days. Some might call it an obsession."

"Well, I'm calling it weird since I've only talked with him. Are you supposed to pay us now?" I ask.

"Yeah, we ain't doing shit until we see the money," Ada says, talking as if she's in some gangster film.

"Shhh," Perry shushes her. "It's not even your money, Ada."

"I have the money right here," Atlas says, pulling an envelope out of his coat. He hands it to me. "Go ahead," he says. "Take a look."

While I open the envelope, Ada says to Atlas. "So, who are you supposed to be for Halloween?"

"Myself," Atlas answers, a lilt to his voice.

"Uh huh," she says. "I thought maybe you were trying to look like Edgar Allan Poe."

"No, no," he says. "Though I am one of his descendants."

I pause to look at him, squinting between him and the check in my hands. "Poe had no children. That's a known fact."

Atlas shrugs. "How could that be known as fact?" He nods at the check. "Does that make sense to you."

It's hard to get a read on the check since the light is so dim, but it does look to be a one followed by six zeros.

My heart skips a beat. I look back at Poe. "How do I know this is any good?"

He gives me a faint smile. "You know, don't you, Dex?"

The hairs at the back of my neck start to rise again, an unsettling feeling in my stomach. I swallow.

He's right. I do know it's real. I can feel it.

I glance at Perry, who is staring at Atlas with a peculiar look on her face, trying to get a read on him too. He's staring right back at her, seeming smug.

He clasps his hands in front of him and then looks to Ada and Jay. "As for you two, you're not part of the original plans. I'm afraid I can't let you in the house."

"What?" Ada exclaims.

"Why not?" asks Perry, both sisters getting worked up.

As for me, I mean, fuck, I have a hundred grand that I'm slipping into my wallet, I couldn't care less what happens after this.

That's not true, I hear an unknown voice snake around in my head. A woman's voice. *You know you want to go inside.*

Go inside.

Go inside.

Oh shit. I press my hands to my temples, trying to stop the voice.

But no one is paying me any attention.

Go inside.

Perry and Ada are trying to argue with Atlas.

Go inside.

Jay is staring at Atlas like he wants to kill him, which is a bit of an overreaction I must say.

Go inside.

And then Atlas' gaze goes to me. A hint of understanding in his eyes.

The voice stops.

"I think we should go inside," I find myself saying. At least, I think that was me saying it.

Perry gives me a look. "Really? Without them?"

"We're the ones who invited them. Well, I did. Harry never knew."

"He just trusts you two," Atlas says. "You understand that you're being invited into his house, to talk to his wife? This is a situation of great reverence. Dex and Perry, you were chosen for a reason."

All the right reasons.

Okay, holy fuck. What is that fucking voice?

I look at Perry and she's staring at me, brows knitting together. It's definitely not her. I glance at Atlas. I don't think it's him either.

Perry reluctantly tears her eyes off me and gives Atlas a sour smile. "Fine. It will be just us two."

"Perry," Ada says. "Come on, we can help."

I expect Jay to say something similar, but he's just standing there, still looking at Atlas like he wants to take his head off and bounce it around for a bit, maybe shoot some hoops with the basketball net on the other side of the street.

Finally, he clears his throat. "It's fine, Ada," he says, grabbing her by the elbow and pulling him toward him.

I have to say, if Jay had said this was a big mistake right now, I wouldn't do it. I would give the money back and call it quits. But he's not saying anything at all. Perhaps his sudden hatred for wannabe Johnny Depp is purely a jealousy thing, I mean, who fucking knows with those ginger bastards anyway.

"Okay then," Atlas says. "Follow me."

He turns and starts walking up the path to the house.

I grab Perry's hand, giving it a squeeze, and then look over at Jay and Ada. "You'll be right here?"

"Not fucking going anywhere," she says. "And if there's anything remotely scary, just call me."

Jeez, when did Little Fifteen get to be such a hot shot in the ghost department?

We nod goodbye to them and then follow Atlas toward the house, going up the creaking front steps. Yes, classic haunted house fixings.

Atlas takes out a skeleton key from his pocket (another nice detail) and opens the interesting door. It groans loudly as he pushes it.

I look back at Khalessi and Outlander boy, who are watching us like hawks.

Atlas steps inside, and I swear the air around him shimmers, just for a second.

Perry squeezes my hand and I gaze down at her.

"Are you ready?" I ask her.

"I think so."

"You gotta be sure, baby. If you don't want to do this, I think this is our only chance to say no. To turn and go. If we walk through that door...I think we're in it. Either we dive in. Or deflect."

"We dive in," she says, giving me a small smile.

We look back to see Atlas standing in the dim interior of the house.

We walk through.

I flinch as we go, expecting to feel the hiss and pop of the Veil, to feel ourselves pulled into a place without color or air.

But nothing happens. We just walk in.

"Mind if I close the door?" Atlas asks, pushing the

heavy door shut. I watch as Ada and Jay disappear. "Don't want this place draftier than it has to be."

I lean over and flick the lights on, but nothing happens.

"There's no electricity," he says to me. "It's been cut off for years."

"That's not true, I saw a light on in the upstairs window," I tell him.

"Did you?" Atlas asks, with a raise of his brow.

I look at Perry. "You saw the light, right?"

She shakes her head. "No, but that doesn't mean anything."

Atlas pulls out a couple of small flashlights from his pocket and hands us each one. "Here, this will do. You know, back in the day I used to give guided tours of this place, so you'll have to pardon me if I revert back into old ways."

He starts walking down the long hall and we follow. "Now, outside you may have noticed the gables and archways as being stylistically medieval English Tudor, while the interior rooms combine elements from various historical styles including Moorish, Romanesque, Gothic, Neoclassical, and Renaissance."

"Sorry, are we actually getting a tour right now?" I ask him, shining my light along the walls. "Because I have to tell you, whenever there's a choice of having a tour guide or going on your own, I always pick the latter."

"I figured," he says with amusement. "I thought you would find it interesting."

The thing is, he *is* kind of right. This house is batshit. It's somehow larger than it looks on the outside with the hallway seeming to stretch forever, ending in a giant, cavernous room. A round arch supported by Romanesque columns frames the view.

"Wow, the ceilings," Perry says in a hush, shining her light up.

The exposed beam ceilings and walls are intricately patterned with painted details, almost mirroring the worn rug that runs down the middle of the hallway. We continue down the hall, the dark room getting closer and closer.

"Where are we going?" I ask, trying not to sound afraid, but there's something about that black, cavernous space that we keep heading toward which makes me feel like my head isn't screwed on straight.

"I'm trying to take you to where my mother was last seen."

"Your mother?" I repeat.

"Last seen? I thought she drowned," says Perry.

He stops and we almost bump into him.

Turns and eyes me. "Yes, Dex, my mother. My mother married Harry after she had me." He looks to Perry. "And yes, she did drown. But the last place she was seen was here. Last Halloween." He points into the room. "Sitting in the dining room."

Chills. I've got motherfucking chills going down my spine.

Hell, it's been a long time since I felt that.

"So, let me get this straight," Perry says. "You believe the same thing as your stepfather."

"Believe?" He purses his lips quizzically.

"Yeah. That her ghost is here."

"Oh. Well, of course her ghost is here. It's been here since the day she died. I see her all the time."

"You do?" I ask, and once again, I don't think the guy is lying.

"That's right," he says with a quick smile, his teeth flashing white. "Why do you think I'm giving you the tour?"

"But then why give us one hundred grand if you can just talk to her for free?"

He laughs, the sound falling flat in this place. "Because my father doesn't trust me. I don't even think he believes me, to be honest. Maybe because I'm too close to her, I don't know. Maybe it's a jealousy thing. Either way, he doesn't want me doing it."

"Not even to pass a message?" I ask.

"Who said anything about passing messages?" Atlas says.

"Your father did," I tell him, getting an uneasy feeling about all of this.

"Oh. I see." He slides a hand into a pocket and shrugs. "If he has a message for her, then I don't know about it. It doesn't matter, he's here all the time yelling at her, even though he rarely sees her himself."

I raise my palm. "Okay, okay. This is getting way beyond the thing that we were told. How do I know that you're not lying to us?"

"You know I'm not."

"Stop fucking acting like I'm supposed to know you, I don't. And you don't fucking know me."

He sighs tiredly, pinching the bridge of his nose. "This isn't the best place for an argument. The more we fight, the more the bad shit will come out."

"Bad shit?" Perry says, her eyes glowing. "Is that a technical term?"

"Tell us why we're really here," I tell him. "Or we're walking." And taking the money, but I don't say that.

He looks us both in the eyes. "Fine. There are no secrets here. My mother is dead, but she hasn't moved on. She... can't. For one reason or another. She's stuck in this house. She just needs a little...push."

"A push?" I ask, narrowing my eyes. "Which way?"

He grins at me. "I suppose that's up to her now. At any rate, my father picked you two because you're somewhat famous and I went along with it because my mother said you would do."

I shake my head. "I don't know what to make of it. What are we supposed to do?"

"He wants us to open the Veil," Perry says quietly. "I won't do it."

Atlas smiles. "You don't need to open the Veil, my dear. It's already open."

I swallow, my body feeling hot and cold. "What do you mean?"

"Samhain," he says. "The most powerful day of the year for a witch. The Veil walls are thin, and in here there are no walls."

That's why I'm here.

The woman's voice slices through my head again, my eyes going wide.

"Dex?" Perry asks in concern.

But I can't move.

My eyes are glued to the space in the dark beyond Atlas.

The graying body of a dead woman slowly disappearing into the black.

Fuck!

"Dex," Perry says again, sharper now.

You'll have to come back, the voice says. *I know how hard that thought gets you.*

Fucking hell, and I do have a fucking erection, don't I?

We'll be here. Waiting.

Then the voice stops and I can move again.

"You okay?" Atlas asks, and luckily no one is pointing their flashlight at my crotch.

"I'm fine," I say, swallowing.

"You look like you saw a ghost," he says, smirking.

"Well I kind of fucking did."

"What did you see?" Perry asks.

"Maybe his mother?" I say, pointing to the dark room where, of course, there's nothing. "I gotta tell you something, I'm not fucking going in there."

Atlas stares into the black for a moment and then nods. "Understood. Come on, I'll give you a tour of the rest of the house."

He walks around us, and even though I don't want a fucking tour, I refuse to be left alone with Perry in this hall. We hurry after him, but the immense darkness at my back feels like a black hole, and if I don't escape from it fast enough, it's going to suck me back in with that dead woman.

"So, wait a minute," Perry says to Atlas, catching up to him. "If the walls are down in this house, why do you need us to do anything?"

"Because I don't have what you guys have," he says, leading us over to the stairs. "Your gift. Just because the Veil is down or thin, doesn't mean spirits will walk through. They might not even know they can. They need to be drawn out. They need to be shown the way. That's what the two of you have always done. That's your purpose in life."

Oh, Perry isn't going to like that.

"Purpose?" she practically spits out as we climb the stairs. "I have a purpose in life and it's not this. It never was."

He glances down at her. "I suppose if you tell yourself that enough times, sooner or later it might be true." He smiles. "But you're here, aren't you?"

"For a fuckload of money!"

"Easy now," he says. "Last time we had words, your husband saw a ghost. Do you want that to happen again?"

"I thought we were here to see ghosts," I tell him as we get to the second floor.

"You're here to talk to my mother," he says. "What you saw wasn't my mother. You definitely don't want to see her again."

"Fucking hell, what else should we not want to see?" I mutter under my breath.

But as Atlas takes us from room to room on the second floor, showing us different bedrooms, still fully furnished, filling us in on some of the seemingly harmless history of the so-called Stimson House, we never see anything else.

That is, until we get to the third floor.

Where I had seen the light from outside.

On that floor I stop dead when I see bloody water seeping out from underneath a doorway.

"Uh," I say, pointing at it, and holy fuck have I never wanted a video camera as bad as I do right now. This is fucking gold.

"Oh my god," Perry says softly, jumping back from the water as it seems to rush toward our feet. "What's in there?" She stares at the door.

"It's a bathroom," Atlas says. "It's locked and I don't have a key."

Oh, this Edgar Allan Fuck is lying, that much is true.

"And it seems we're out of time," he says, taking out his phone.

"What do you—?" My words are cut off by all the lights in the house going on at once.

Illuminating people standing all around us.

Dead people.

Fucking *everywhere*.

Perry and I scream bloody murder, our voices rattling through the house.

And then the lights go back off.

The dead people disappear.

The bloody water that was inches from my boots, retreats back under the door, like a film in reverse.

"November first," Atlas says tiredly. "The walls have closed."

I barely hear him, barely take in how quickly time has passed while we've been in this house.

All I hear is the rush of blood in my head.

The dry rasp of my breath as I try to breathe.

And all I feel is something deep inside me coming alive again, hitching a ride on the adrenaline that's pumping through my veins.

I look down at Perry to see if she feels it too, the electricity, the heat, the desire. The...purpose. Because fuck it if Atlas wasn't right about that.

She's breathing hard, her hand to her chest and she looks scared.

Really wish that didn't turn me on so much, but this house has fucked with me a bunch of different ways already.

And I want more.

I glance over at Atlas to see him watching me with curiosity, a gleam in his eye.

He knows. He knows what I have planned.

That's why he brought us here.

"So," he says carefully. "I'll have to tell my father that it didn't quite work this time."

"This time?" Perry asks, giving her head a little shake. "No, we only agreed to this one time."

"You won't come back another night? I don't think you'll have any problems getting through." He pauses, licking his lips. "Or are you just going to take the money and call it quits?"

"That's not fair," Perry says. She looks at me expectantly. "Dex? We're not doing this again."

But didn't you feel it? Didn't you feel plugged into the motherfucking universe?

I'm not sure if she hears me or not.

"We'll think about it," I tell Atlas, even though he knows I've already made up my mind. "Give us a few days."

"Take all the time you want," he says. "She'll stay dead forever."

What a callous way to think about your own mother, then again, I've thought that and worse about my own. Perhaps Atlas and I have more in common than I thought.

We make our way down the stairs, and I hold onto Perry's hand the whole time to give her reassurance for the time being.

Then Atlas opens the front door and we step outside into the night. The air smiles like firecrackers again, it's cold as hell, and I feel like every sense I have is suddenly heightened.

Ada and Jay are at the bottom of the steps and Ada immediately rushes toward us, pulling Perry into a hug. "Oh my god, are you okay?" she cries out. "We saw all the lights in the house go on. I saw a fucking ghost boy in the window!"

"Yeah, we, uh, saw all that," Perry says.

We walk down the steps and then Atlas gives a nod, like he's some old timey gentleman saying goodbye. "Let me know when you want to talk," he says, and then he goes down the street, disappearing around the corner as quickly as he had appeared earlier.

"What the fuck was that?" Jay asks me. "That fucking house is not a house, is it?"

"I don't know what that was," Perry says. "I just want to get the hell out of here."

"Oh, let's go back to that hotel and get more drinks." Ada claps her hands together, apparently able to turn from "I saw a ghost boy" to "More underage drinking!" in a heartbeat. "Do you think they're still open?"

"Princess, it's past midnight," Jay says, putting his arm around her. "And we have our own hotel to get to."

She grins at him, remembering.

We start walking down the street back the way we came, and the further we get from that house, the less of a pull it has on me. By the time we're at the Sorrento Hotel and calling an Uber, it almost feels like a dream, like none of it happened at all.

But I know it happened.

I know what I saw.

I know what I felt.

And I know that I'll be back.

With my camera next time.

THE END

   ...or...the beginning...

HAVE YOU HEARD THE GOOD NEWS? THIS STORY continues on in CAME BACK HAUNTED, the all-new full-length novel, Experiment in Terror #10. Releasing on December 11th, 2020.

Dex & Perry are back, baby! Make sure to join me on social media for all the latest updates.

OH and be sure to keep reading for TARGET, a Dex & Perry short story that I wrote waaaaay back in the day, when Perry first moves in with Dex (around Into The Hollow times).

TARGET

A DEX & PERRY SHORT STORY

There's nothing like waking up to having your toes licked. In fact, when done by the right pair of lips, it's just as good as having your morning wood primed and pumped. Unfortunately, I knew my toes weren't being licked by the girl in the room next door. It was the damn fucking dog. Again.

"Fuck off," I mumbled into my pillow and shook my foot. Fat Rabbit had been sleeping with Perry for the last few nights, so my morning-addled brain couldn't figure out why the bastard was in here anyway, munching away on my toes like they were doggy popsicles.

Then I heard a supressed giggle.

I slowly raised my head and looked over at the door. Perry was standing there like some heavenly wet dream. I mean, she was *wet*. Her hair was cascading down her face like inky trails, beads of water glistening on her shoulders and collarbones as she clutched my tiny towel to her chest. I'd never been so happy to have such woefully undersized towels in my life. It turns out she didn't feel the same way.

"Dex," she said, eying me with impatience, as if the fact

that I was still in bed at 10a.m. was just the tip of the iceberg. "You need new towels."

I sat up, not caring how close I was to being fully exposed by my duvet cover. Two could play at this barely concealing ourselves game and from the way her eyes were fighting to stay at my face and not drift down to the poke-your-eye-out zone, we were evenly matched.

"My towels are just fine," I told her as Fat Rabbit made a futile attempt to jump on the bed. "Is this your not-so subtle attempt to seduce me, because I have to say it's working."

She rolled her eyes and tried to tighten the towel around her chest. Her chest argued back. "I can seduce you just by tying my shoes."

"It's because when you're bending over, I get a great view no matter where I am," I said with a wag of my eyebrow. Man, I loved annoying her.

Her eyes narrowed briefly, but I knew she was loving it. At least, I hoped she was. I could never be too sure these days, especially since I was still in the proverbial dog house. I guess it was fitting that Fatty Rab was in the same room as me, farting up a storm.

"Look," she said, leaning against the doorframe. Oh, I was looking. "I've been living here for long enough and if I'm seriously going to be your roommate for the next little while, I have to make my influence felt."

I had to admit, it stung a bit when she emphasised "little while." There was nothing I wanted more than to Perry to just put her roots down here, in this apartment with me, where she belonged. But it seemed like less and less of a possibility as the days went on. My attempts to win her over, to win her back, were shoved away by whatever damage I had inflicted on her heart.

"Okay," I said and decided to get serious. I pulled up the blanket around my waist and looked at her straight-on. "You know I'll do whatever you want to make you more comfortable here. Is it just the towels?"

A small smile tugged at the corner of her lips. Damn, she was fucking beautiful without a stitch of makeup or pretention. These moments, like the ones before, always caught me off guard, always reminded me of what a fucking mess I had created and the garbage disposal I was falling in.

"No, it's not just the towels," she said lightly. "But it's a start. They're like a million years old and been air-dried one too many times. Not to mention their size. Maybe it worked to be parading around half-naked with Jenn, but it's not going to be the same with me."

Damn. A Jenn mention combined with a rejection uppercut. She wasn't playing very nice this morning. Round and round the disposal I went.

"All right," I conceded, wiping my eyes awake. "We need new towels. Anything else?"

"New bedsheets, not the ones you borrowed from Rebecca. Something nice for the room. I'd also like a small chest of drawers for my clothes, maybe something charming for my jewelry and shit."

"That can be arranged," I said. "You know, if you want you can move in this room. I have no problems sleeping in the den. This can be your room from now on."

A wash of sadness came over her blue eyes. Her gaze fixed on the floor. "No, thank you, but I like the den. I've slept there before...it's the only place that really feels like home to me now, you know?"

I did. "They opened up a Target downtown recently, want to go check it out?"

That put another smile on her face. I fucking hated

Target with a passion, but I'd gladly endure the blank-faced, jogging pants and screaming children, soulless money-trap to see those dimples again and again.

∼

Target was the newest blemish on downtown Seattle's increasingly gentrified face. It was like the city said, "Sure, suburbs, come rest your fat asses on our gritty, thought-provoking pores, we don't mind."

I regretfully expressed this very sentiment to Perry and she told me I was nothing but a hipster. Ouch. She was really going all out today.

Luckily, Perry isn't as wiffle-waffley as you'd think when it comes to shopping. Ask her about her favorite band, her favorite movie, or how she feels about one Dex Foray and you'd get a million different, indecisive answers. But once Perry hit the glaring lights of the fluorescent showroom of death, she was sucked straight toward the homewares department like she was in their tractor beam. Ten minutes later, the red shopping cart was drowning in a sea of fluffy towels that I swore were made out of poodles, a silky blue bedset, a faux-wooden set of drawers that looked like they were salvaged from IKEA rejects and frou-frou girly things that made my head spin. I had to give her credit; in this case, she knew exactly what she wanted and she was getting it.

"Wow," I said, leaning oh-so casually against the cart's handlebars as she piled in a bunch of smelly candles. "Now that you've put a whole sweatshop back in business, do you need anything else? Lingerie, perhaps?"

She snorted and started walking down the aisle, her boots squeaking. "You'd like that wouldn't you?"

I shrugged and pushed the cart along. "Not really for

myself. I find thongs are a bit too binding around my balls. I need gentle cupping action, not dental floss down the seam."

"That's a shame," she said over her shoulder. "I think you'd pull off pink lace very nicely."

I wished I had a rebuttal for that, but all I could think about was her in something pink and lacey. Perry was one of those girls who was built to fuck. I know, I know, it sounds crude and maybe it is, but there's something extremely poetic about it. She thinks she's heavy and plus-sized, but she's perfectly sized. She's short enough that I can just pick her up and show her who's the boss. Yet with her hips, her curves, those fan-fuckingtastic breasts, she's the one who calls all the shots. She's oblivious to the power she has over men and it was only recently that she began to clue into the power she has over me.

It's too bad she doesn't know what to do with it.

She slowed down, the sexy sashay of her walk keeping my eyes glued to her ass, then she suddenly ducked down one of the aisles. It was the pet department. Not exactly where we needed to go.

"Perry," I warned.

"I'm seeing if there's something cute for Fat Rabbit," she said, stopping near the shirts.

"Don't you dare," I said, ramming the cart against her ass. As I suspected, it bounced right off.

"Ow," she said absently as she went through the racks of embarrassing dog outfits. Hey, I loved Fat Rabbit as much as a guy can love a small, furry poop-machine, but there was no way in hell any dog of mine was going to look like slobbering Honey Boo Boo.

"I know I said you could make yourself feel more comfortable, it just can't be at the expense of my dog's comfort. Fatty Rab will hate you if you put him in any of these shirts."

"Oh, whatever," she said dismissively, examining a polka dot parka. "Fatty Rab can tell me himself, plus it's still winter. It's cold out."

"You can justify it anyway you want," I said shaking my head, "but – "

"Mommy!" a Nazgul-ish shriek emitted from the other side of Perry.

We both looked over. A tiny, sniveling little boy of about three or four years old was running toward Perry with his arms open wide. This was a new development.

She stared down at the boy, afraid and perplexed until the boy stopped a couple feet away and looked at her with a matching expression.

"You're not my mommy," the boy whimpered. Poor little fucker.

Perry immediately put the parka back on the rack and crouched down to the boy's level.

"Are you lost?" she asked, her voice soaring to sugary heights that made my heart pang.

The boy wiped his nose and his eyes, smearing snot all over his face. Yet, Perry soothingly patted the boys head as if the snot wasn't there. I had to admit, seeing her act like a mother-in-training was actually gutwrenching. It made me think of things that I tried so damn hard not to think about.

"I think so," the boy said. "I want my mommy."

She continued to pat the boy on the head, taking his hand in hers. "Well, I'm not your mommy but I'm sure I can find her for you. Would you like me to do that?"

The kid sniffled and nodded.

"What's your name?"

"Tyler," he squeaked out.

She gave him a kind smile then looked over at me.

"Dex, can you look after him while I find his mother?"

Uh. Fuck no?

"Don't look so scared," she hissed under her breath, glaring at me while she led the boy my way. I felt like I was stuck to the ground. "He needs to stay here in case his mother is looking for him."

My mouth flapped open but no sounds came out. Perry deposited the boy at my feet and the two of us stared at each other uneasily.

She quickly patted me on the shoulder and with the same soothing tone she had given the Nazgul, said, "I'm just going to the cashier to let them make an announcement, I'll be right back."

And just like that, Perry left and I was put in charge of some stranger's snotty, strange child.

A child that was starting to cry again.

"So your name is Tyler, huh?" I said in an extremely feeble attempt at conversation. "That's a good name."

Tyler continued to cry. He was starting to attract the attention of people passing by. This wouldn't look good. I was wearing a Black Flag t-shirt and combat boots. My expression was of a million jangled nerves begging for respite. My mustache was starting to grow back in. I might as well start talking about the giant white van I had outside, full of candy.

But kids liked candy, didn't they?

"Tyler," I said, crouching down, trying to look him in the eye. "You like candy don't you?"

He sniffled some more and wiped his nose on his sleeve. Nasty.

"What's your favorite candy?" I went on.

Tyler thought about it. For once, he looked calm. In fact,

he looked like he was in his element, picking out the sugary sweets that would lead to his early on-set diabetes.

"I like Whatchamcalits," he said. Which was a total lie, since the only reason people liked Whatchamacalits were because of the name. "And Butterfingers."

"Nobody better lay a finger on my Butterfinger," I said in my best Bart Simpson voice. Okay, now the kid was looking at me like I grew an extra head. I pitied the generation who grew up without Bart as a role model. "All right, how about I promise you all the Whatchamacalits and Butterfingers in the world, if you stop crying and start manning up."

"Do you have a doggie?" he asked, ignoring me, his eyes now focused on the pet stuff around us.

"Uh, yes," I said, somewhat proudly. "His name is Fat Rabbit."

"I want to see him," Tyler said, sounding more forceful by the second. He even stamped his foot a little.

"Well, how about we wait for your mommy and then I can take you back to my apartment where you can pet my dog and I'll give you lots of candy?"

"Really?" he cried out, his smile wide and all gap-toothed.

I straightened up. "Uh, yeah, totally." Oh, I was going to hell.

"Mommy!" Tyler suddenly cried out and barreled past me. I whipped around to see a pregnant young mom in purple velour and bling staring at me utterly horrified. She held her arm out for Tyler, who jumped into her, wrapping himself around her leg.

"Who the hell are you?" she asked, a stack of magazines in her red basket. "What the hell were you doing with my son?"

She had all the tact of a viper. I immediately raised my hands in defense and starting cursing Perry for leaving me alone with the munchkin.

"It's okay, I was just getting to know Tyler here," I told her. Apparently I worded it wrong, because her eyes narrowed into reptilian slits and I knew I was about to get bitten.

"What were you doing with my son?" she asked again, spitting out the words like ninja stars.

I tried to put on my most handsome face, which usually worked with women. Not with her though.

"He was lost, my girlfriend...well, no my friend. Roomate. My partner! Yes, my partner, she went to go get help, to see if we could find you." I could not sound stupider if I tried.

"Mommy," Tyler tugged at her terry-cloth sweatshirt, "Mommy, he told me he's going to take me away for some candy and I can pet his fat dog."

The next thing I knew, a handbag came swinging at my face. I only had seconds to react. I did not use those seconds wisely. The handbag in all its Guess monogrammed glory met with my forehead and I nearly went flying into the row of dog parkas.

"You sick freak!" the woman shrieked. By the time I could straighten myself and see again, she was gone, storming down the aisle in a huff, her Nazgul a leech at her side.

And there was Perry, passing by them with a smile on her face. They did not return the smile. She shrugged and kept walking, stopping in front of me.

"What happened to you?" she asked, completely amused. Not one ounce of sincere sympathy.

Now it was my turn to glare. "What happened? You left

me in charge of Satan's spawn and then Satan herself showed up, that's what. I thought you were going to make an announcement."

She was trying really hard not to laugh, her hand at her mouth. "I was, but the line was so long and I saw them together, so..."

I shook my head. "Figures."

She punched me lightly on the shoulder. "And here I was under the impression that my roommate was a ladies' man."

"You've caught me on a bad day," I told her smoothing my hair back. We got out of Target before some other mothers could accuse me trying to corrupt their children. Perhaps I wasn't the biggest ladies' man that Perry had thought I was, but at least she called me her roommate. And for now, being any kind of mate of hers, was good enough for me.

ABOUT THE AUTHOR

Karina Halle is a screenwriter, a former music & travel journalist, and the *New York Times*, *Wall Street Journal*, and *USA Today* bestselling author of *The Pact*, *A Nordic King*, and *Sins & Needles*, as well as sixty other wild and romantic reads.

She, her musician husband, and their adopted pit bull, Bruce, live in a rainforest on an island off the coast of British Columbia, where they operate Raven Ridge, a B&B that's perfect for writers' retreats and romantic getaways.

In the winter, you can often find them in California or on their beloved island of Kauai, soaking up as much sun (and getting as much inspiration) as possible. For more information, visit www.authorkarinahalle.com/books.

ALSO BY KARINA HALLE

Contemporary Romances

Love, in English

Love, in Spanish

Where Sea Meets Sky

Racing the Sun

The Pact

The Offer

The Play

Winter Wishes

The Lie

The Debt

Smut

Heat Wave

Before I Ever Met You

After All

Rocked Up

Wild Card (North Ridge #1)

Maverick (North Ridge #2)

Hot Shot (North Ridge #3)

Bad at Love

The Swedish Prince

The Wild Heir

A Nordic King

Nothing Personal

My Life in Shambles

The Royal Rogue

The Forbidden Man

Lovewrecked

One Hot Italian Summer

The One That Got Away

Romantic Suspense Novels by Karina Halle

Sins and Needles (The Artists Trilogy #1)

On Every Street (An Artists Trilogy Novella #0.5)

Shooting Scars (The Artists Trilogy #2)

Bold Tricks (The Artists Trilogy #3)

Dirty Angels (Dirty Angels #1)

Dirty Deeds (Dirty Angels #2)

Dirty Promises (Dirty Angels #3)

Black Hearts (Sins Duet #1)

Dirty Souls (Sins Duet #2)

Discretion (The Dumonts #1)

Disarm (The Dumonts #2)

Disavow (The Dumonts #3)

Horror Romance

Darkhouse (EIT #1)

Red Fox (EIT #2)

The Benson (EIT #2.5)

VEILED

In the event that you haven't read Veiled yet, here are the first few chapters to whet your appetite.

CHAPTER ONE

I wake up with a gasp that freezes in my lungs.

My body is strained, nearly paralyzed, a stark contrast to my heart which races erratically inside my chest, as if looking for a way out.

It was the noise that woke me.

That same noise, night after night.

One knock.

Two knocks.

Three knocks.

Like someone's at my door, even though they never are.

I wait, trying to suck the air deep into my lungs, realizing I couldn't move even if I tried. There's nothing else to do but wait and hope my heart calms down and I don't die from a fucking heart attack.

It's in your head, I tell myself. *You know this. You looked it up.*

But after growing up with a sister like Perry Palomino, it's hard to know what's in your head and what's real. I much prefer it when my mind plays tricks on me.

Even so, I lie there in the dark, listening to every sound in my room. Outside a cricket chirps once, twice. A light breeze rustles the trees and I feel the air as it comes through the open window and washes over my body, my limbs that are outside the sheets. It's been stinking hot in Portland this summer and this breeze is nearly cold. It would be refreshing if I wasn't so rattled.

Strength slowly returns to my body. I'm able to suck in a breath and let it out carefully, even though it's far too loud for my liking. I'm still trying to listen, still trying to figure out if the knocks are part of my dream or part of something real.

I've had this condition for about as long as I can remember, though it was only recently that I looked it up and discovered it was quite common. It also has a disturbing as hell name: Exploding Head Syndrome. Yup. Ada Palomino's head might explode on occasion. Hope you're wearing a poncho.

Apparently though, it's not that big of a deal and it doesn't mean your head is just going to spontaneously combust, like that dude in *Scanners*. Now, I've never seen *Scanners* because it looks like a terrible 80's movie, but anytime someone's head explodes, that's the movie they refer to.

Instead it just means it's an auditory hallucination, one powerful enough to wake you up. Some people hear cymbals crashing, others hear a bang or gunshot. I hear three loud knocks. I used to think it was someone at my door, so I would get up and answer it, thinking it was Perry. No one was ever there. Sometimes I'd have to go downstairs and check the front door, usually with a steak knife or blunt object in hand, but it was always the same deal.

No one there.

Then this spring, when I slept over at my ex-boyfriend's cabin in Astoria, I woke up convinced someone was trying to get in the place. My ex, Dillon, was already awake, having gone to the washroom and told me he hadn't heard a thing.

Finally, I had to look up on the internet what the hell was going on. I discovered it had a name (albeit a pretty shitty one) and that many people suffered from it, usually women and usually when they were overly tired.

I've had it a few times since, but sometimes it's just so real that it's hard to imagine your brain could come up with something like that. Not to mention that often my body goes rigid, paralyzed, for a few moments after.

Then there was that one time I was pretty sure I felt someone sitting on the end of the bed, only I was on my side and couldn't look.

The weight lifted, as if someone stood up, and when I was finally able to move, no one was there. I'm going to assume that's part of the hallucinations as well.

I sigh, relieved that my heart is no longer racing, even though I'm still faced with that overall sense of unease and *what the fuck.* My throat and mouth feel desert dry, so I slowly get out of bed, grabbing the empty glass on my bedside table, and head to the washroom. The air from outside now feels warm, like it has been all summer.

In the bathroom I flick on the lights and wince, but make a point not to look at myself in the mirror. On nights like this, when I wake up in the middle of the night, either because of my apparent condition or for no reason at all, other than this feeling of dread, I feel the mirror holds the truth. I'm terrified that if I look at my reflection, it might not be me. And if it is me, I might be different.

But who can blame me for thinking the impossible? Because, after all I've been through, I know nothing is impossible. And even though on the surface I have a pretty average life for an eighteen-year-old, beneath the surface I'm anything but average.

Luckily, very few people scratch beneath the surface. If they did, they'd either run screaming or have me committed.

Sometimes I think the latter might be preferable.

After I fill a glass with water from the tap, I flick off the lights, my reflection still unseen, and creep past the night-light in the hall back to my room. My father sleeps at the end of the hall, but ever since mom died he's been a light sleeper. In fact, I see him popping his sleeping pills every night. When he doesn't, I can hear him downstairs in his study during all hours.

I inherited my sister's room since she moved to Seattle. It's a lot bigger, brighter, and better than my old one, which is now a (much-needed) extension of my closet. The only problem is, it's hard to forget all the shit that went down in this room. For all of my fifteenth year, Perry's bedroom was a miniature house of horrors with some very big, very real, scares.

I down some of the water and crawl into bed, the breeze still wafting in. The streetlights provide comfort and a faint orange glow that not only keeps the room from being pitch dark, but reminds me that I live in the suburbs. There are neighbors on either side of the house and neighbors across the street. Our yards are big enough that everyone isn't up in everyone else's business (though tell that to Mrs.

Hedley down the street), but close enough that I don't feel all alone.

With my mom dying and Perry moving out, it's been really fucking hard not to feel alone. The last two years have been a special kind of hell.

I let my head sink back into the cool of the pillow and close my eyes, finding that current of peace and contentment that will hopefully pull me under, when I hear a faint scratching sound.

Oh god, I think, just wanting to drift away, just wanting the world to go black so I can wake up with the sun and have the world light again.

But it goes on. Not louder, just more . . . deliberate.

I slowly sit up and hold my breath, listening. The scratches sound like nails against a door. The closet door, to be more specific.

I swallow hard and my heart begins to thud. It's not my imagination. I'm not asleep.

The sound continues, the strokes longer, the sound succinct, almost echoing throughout the bedroom.

It could be a mouse. A really large mouse. Okay, it could be a rat. A really large rat. God, I hope it's a rat. If it's a rat it can just stay in there until I get my dad to deal with it in the morning. Anything other than some type of animal is completely unacceptable.

I ease out of bed carefully, not making a sound, and stare at the closet, feeling frozen in place. There's no way in hell I'm opening that door, but there's no way in hell I'm going to spend the night in here either. I wonder if I should wake up my dad, but the man needs his sleep more than ever and knowing my luck, the scratching would stop when he gets here and there'd be nothing in the closet after all.

I'll sleep in the other room.

I can't help but pause by the closet on the way to the bedroom door.

The sound changes. A flurry of wings now, flapping against the closet door, the scratching louder.

My breath is caught in my throat. It sounds more like I have a chicken in the closet than a mutant rat, but even though I know there's something funny about that scenario, this doesn't seem funny at all.

Because a giant rat is plausible and a chicken is not.

And the wings don't exactly sound like feathers either.

The flapping is thick, like someone throwing slabs of raw meat against a wall.

I am zero seconds away from either vomiting from fear or literally losing my shit, but if I keep standing where I am I feel like I'll be stuck in the room forever.

And then I hear it.

A rough yet somehow familiar voice comes from the closet.

"Let me out," it croaks and the sound is a fist in my lungs.

The closet door rattles as someone on the other side knocks.

Three times.

I wake up.

~

"New purse?" Amy asks me as I get in the passenger seat of Smartie, her Ford Focus she bought second-hand a few months ago after saving every pretty penny.

I look down at the micro YSL bubble-gum pink purse that's slung over my shoulder, which I chose to save up for instead of a car.

"Kind of," I tell her. I bought the purse on an online sale a couple of months ago, I just hadn't found the opportunity to wear it until now. I buy new things all the time—I mean, I'm a fashion blogger, it's kind of my job—but more often than not I get stuck in the habit of using the same bag over and over again.

Today though, today I needed some cheesy bubble-gum brightness in my life. I'd been having the worst sleep for the last few nights, ever since that dream upon a dream and the knocking and the chicken thing in the closet. Thankfully I hadn't experienced that again, even though I was giving my closet a wide berth now. The irony, that I'd be afraid of it when I'm about to start art school for fashion design next month and would probably be spending more time in my closet than ever before, wasn't lost on me.

But I had been dreaming about a guy I met once, and in some ways those dreams were worse. I'd wake up in this happy, warm state, like my heart was glowing and I was just floating through life. The opposite of waking up from a nightmare. Because even though I couldn't remember the specifics of the dreams, I knew I was with this guy and I was safe and I loved him. I couldn't even tell if he loved me back, it was just this feeling of being on top of the world, something I'd never really experienced.

And that's what made it worse. When you wake up from a nightmare, the reality comforts you. When you wake up from the best dream ever, reality is a burden, a slap-in-the-face reminder that you could feel this, you could have this, but you don't and you won't.

What's really weird is that I can't really recall the guy. Like in most dreams, he starts off as one person and then morphs. I lose focus. But I just have this image, this feeling, that he was this guy I met at Perry and her husband Dex's wedding two years ago (still weird to think of Dex as her husband—my brother-in-law—and not some douchecanoe that hangs around).

His name was Jay and I really wish I hadn't swigged so much champagne at the wedding because, just like the dream, the real-life details of him are kind of blurry. I know he was tall, maybe in his mid-to-late-twenties, which to my then sixteen-year-old-self seemed all sorts of ancient. He had reddish brown hair and manly scruff on his strong jaw. I'm not really sure why I think I know the feel of his rough stubble—I think if we kissed I would have at least remembered that.

Regardless, there was something about him that was vaguely magnetic and, considering my aversion to gingers, that said something. And what it said was that the last time I felt real butterflies around a guy was ages ago, I was drunk, and I never saw him again. How sad is that?

"Are you okay?" Amy asks as we head across the Fremont Bridge, the Willamette River sparkling below us.

I slide my eyes over to her and give her a tepid smile. "I'm heading to Sephora. Of course I'm okay."

Amy Lombardo is pretty much my closest friend. She's been there for me through everything from losing my virginity with Dillon (okay, she wasn't actually there for *that*, but she helped me deal with the aftermath), to breakups, to cramming for final exams. She, along with her boyfriend Tom and our friend Jessie, make up our little posse that has managed to last throughout the crazy high school years and now into this scary big world of the beyond. Jessie has already gone off to school in California, so our pack has dwindled to me being the third wheel most of the time.

Amy takes her eyes off the road and slides her

sunglasses down on her nose, inspecting me with her chocolate brown eyes. "You sure?"

Her voice is soft and I know she's worried about me. The first year after my mother died, I was practically inconsolable. I'm surprised I even finished high school to be honest. Life was just a blur and when it wasn't a blur, when I was feeling things too deeply, too much, I made it a blur. I never thought I'd follow in my sister's footsteps, but I turned to drugs and alcohol in order to get through the days.

But the nights were always worst. The drugs never helped me with the nights. The dreams would come for me, no matter how doped up or drunk I was.

Somehow I got out of it. The days seemed brighter, steadier. When I hurt, which was all the time, which still is all the time, I was able to absorb it, deal with it. I was able to think, to actually see myself, my life, and distance myself from the substances. I leaned on Perry, my father, even Dex. Amy, Tom, and Jessie were there too. My ex bailed when I was too much of a mess, but he was just extra baggage anyway. The heartbreak over losing him was nothing compared to losing my mom.

I know Amy worries about me still. I know I'm not the same person I was before it happened. It doesn't help that Amy doesn't know the truth about how my mother died. The truth about me. The truth about my family.

I need to keep it that way. I've seen what our ghostly afflictions can do to someone. I know that my grandmother, Pippa, saw dead people and could enter a realm called the Thin Veil, and that in time she was committed and eventually died alone because no one believed her. I know that Perry has been haunted since she was fifteen, that she was put on a cocktail of medications that did no good, that the world wanted to lock her up because it didn't understand her. I know that my mother saw the truth—far too late.

And the truth killed her.

Even my brother-in-law comes from a lineage of fucked-upness. Dex was also plagued by ghosts from a young age, did a stint in a mental institution, and relied on medication to keep it all away. When he went off the meds—and had his infamous ghost-hunting show with Perry—things only got worse until he discovered his own brother was taken over by a demon and literally tried to take us all to Hell while we were in New York. Worst vacation ever.

Then there's me. I've seen so much, been through so much, that even if I did admit to my best friend that my sister's now defunct ghost-hunting show was totally true, that I've seen the world behind the curtain, I've seen exorcisms and monsters and the devil himself, I wouldn't know where to begin nor how to make it all sound remotely believable.

So I let Amy think that I'm tired and on edge because I'm still grieving and not because my dreams keep getting worse and worse and I feel like each day is leading me down a dark path I might not be able to come back from.

"I'm fine," I tell Amy, loudly, struck by the sudden need to convince myself of this as well. I quickly reach over and shut off the annoying poppy shit on the radio and flip to my favorite alternative station.

When Nine Inch Nails comes on, Amy makes a sound of disgust. "So now you think One Direction sucks?" She rolls her eyes, clearly not amused as we take the exit to downtown. "You really are turning into your sister, you know?"

In more ways than one, I think to myself. But even though Amy chides my sudden change in music tastes and

I'm becoming a bona fide 90's grunge and metal lover even though I was born at the end of that decade, I'm not ashamed of it. I look up to Perry, more than she'll probably ever know. Besides, seeing ghosts and demons just lends itself to listening to White Zombie and Slayer and Fantomas on repeat. One Direction and Selena Gomez are for the girls who don't see dead people every fucking day.

Not that I was seeing dead people every day. I mean, maybe I do, but half the time you don't really realize it unless they're covered in blood, or maybe standing in a white dress in the middle of a road, like every cliché you can think of. Most of the time, the dead just kind of . . . blend in. They're innocuous and usually harmless. Sure they can scare the pants off you but that's usually the extent of their damage.

I gaze out the window as we roll through the Pearl District, watching the throngs of people on the sidewalks, everyone in shorts and tank-tops and billowy dresses, trying to beat the heat.

Then, for just a second, I see a flash of a familiar face as he gets off a bus. I straighten up and blink, trying to see better but he's gone.

It couldn't have been the guy from the wedding, the guy from my dreams, could it? God, I really am getting delusional.

When we finally find parking and I'm swallowed by my mecca that is Sephora, I'm feeling better. There's nothing like sipping on syrupy Coca-Cola from the mall's food court while perusing the white, backlit-beauty of a million makeup products. It's like being in heaven, really, if angels wore all black and enough foundation to paint a house.

Amy and I literally spend an hour here, trying on everything and filling our baskets until our lips are rubbed raw from the makeup remover and our hands and wrists are rainbows of different swatches.

Then it happens.

I see him again.

Standing just beyond the doors to the store.

Staring right at me.

And for once, for once, I can see him clearly.

He's tall, well over six feet. Broad shouldered and barrel-chested under a black leather jacket and black shirt, black jeans and black boots. He's pale in a way that brings to mind a classical sculpture, or maybe it's his face, which is exactly as my mind has tried to piece together.

His jaw is chiseled, his chin square and sharp enough to cut glass, covered by light scruff and complete with a chin dimple. His forehead is wide, expressive even, as he stares at me with piercing blue eyes under arched brows. His hair is chin length, slicked off his head, dark cinnamon. A ginger, just as I had remembered, though he's probably the sexiest, most enthralling male specimen I've ever seen.

"Can I help you with anything?" a Sephora saleswoman with stripes for cheekbones steps in front of me, blocking my view.

I shoot her a dirty look, because I *never* need help in Sephora, and dart around her.

But he's gone.

I hand the bewildered assistant my bucket and walk quickly through the store until I'm outside the doors, my head whipping around. People are going to and fro but the tall guy from my dreams, *from my fucking dreams*, is nowhere to be found.

Maybe he was never here at all.

Suddenly I'm hit with a queasy, stomach-churning feeling, my skin immediately clammy.

"Ada!" Amy calls from behind me but her words barely reach.

I can only just stand here, shoppers walking past me, bumping into me, wondering if I'm slowly going insane. Am I actually seeing this guy? Is it one of those cases where you dream about someone and then see them the next day? Is he really the guy from the wedding or was there even a Jay at all? Did I imagine everything?

I'm having trouble standing upright and tilt back just as I feel Amy's hand on my shoulder, holding me up.

"Hey, are you all right?"

I nod, licking my parched lips as I slowly turn around to face her. Everything seems so swimmy, woozy, like I'm underwater.

"Got dizzy," I manage to say. "It's the Coke crash."

She frowns at me. "Why are you out here?"

I blink a few times, trying to get my thoughts together. "Nothing. Thought I saw someone but it was nothing." I take in a deep breath and give her a broad smile. "Okay, I think I've got some makeup waiting for me."

We head back into the store.

CHAPTER TWO

My head is still swimming when Amy drops me off at home and I blame it on getting my period rather than the mysterious dream man I saw in town. I give her a wave with my Sephora bags and watch her drive off, standing next to the For Sale sign on our front lawn.

I hate that our house is for sale. It adds another level of uncertainty to my life, not knowing if I'm going to spend half my school year here, or in an apartment with a roommate I don't know. I know the market is slow right now and my dad is asking for a bit much, maybe because deep down he doesn't want to move either, but our neighbors sold their house in just a month, so who knows what will happen.

Speaking of neighbors, one of my new ones has spotted me as she exits her house, the driveway full of boxes. They only moved in yesterday, a retired couple, who had a group of brawny movers helping them and providing mucho eye candy as I watched through my bedroom window.

Normally I would march right into my house and feign ignorance, but with my mom gone someone has to step up as woman of the house.

"Hello," the woman says to me, coming over to the fence and holding a pan of what looks like brownies. She's gorgeous even though she has to be in her mid-sixties. Her hair is curly and pulled back, a stunning shade of grey, and her face is pale and freckled giving her a youthful appearance.

I walk over to her and smile, always feeling a bit awkward in these types of situations. You know, the ones that require being polite and normal.

"Hi," I tell her. "You must be our new neighbors."

Well. Duh. Good one, Ada.

"We are," she says, smiling with perfect teeth. "I'm Dawn." She offers her hand and I reach over the low fence to give it a light shake.

"Ada," I tell her.

She nods over at the For Sale sign. "Though perhaps we won't be your neighbors for long."

I sigh. "Yeah, believe me I'd rather not move."

"Lived here long?"

"My whole life," I tell her, feeling my heart pinch. I swallow and attempt a shrug. "Though I am starting college next month so I guess it's time for me to hit the road anyway. My older sister moved out and it's just my dad and me." I don't know why I'm blabbing on to this woman but there's something about her that makes me think she'd understand. I pause. "My mom died a few years ago and I think the house just holds too many memories."

Her face softens. "I'm so sorry. That must be so tough. I lost my mother when I was younger . . . you never quite get over it."

Great. But hell. At least she's telling me the truth. Everyone else makes it sound like death is something you forget with time.

"Here," she says, passing the brownies over the fence. "I'm not the best cook even after all these years, but you can bet I can bake the shit out of brownies."

I can't help but smile. I like her already. I take the pan, the Sephora bags sliding down my arms. "Thanks. These aren't special brownies, are they?"

She laughs. "No, I'm sorry. But those are my specialty too. My husband and I moved from Washington so we're used to being knee-deep in pot brownies on the regular." She tilts her head as she looks at me and I feel like she's really taking me in, seeing everything. "You should come over sometime. I mean, I know it's probably the last thing a girl like you wants to do, hang out with a bunch of old geezers. But I promise you we're fun. Do you like music?"

I frown. "Who doesn't like music?"

She shrugs. "Weirdos."

The perfect answer.

I'm about to tell her that would be great, though I'm not sure if I'd actually follow through with it or not, when an old beige Mercedes pulls up to their curb and Dawn turns her attention to it.

A tall man wearing sunglasses and a baseball cap comes

out of the car and strolls toward us, holding a bouquet of flowers. I wonder if this is her husband.

"You're early," Dawn says to him.

"Your new house is easier to find than I thought," the man says, speaking in a thick Cockney accent. "Lovely though. I was getting a bit tired of that dustbowl you were living in before."

Okay, definitely not her husband. The man stops in front of me and I can almost feel his gaze beneath his sunglasses. He's probably in his fifties, a craggy yet charismatic face, crooked smile, with red hair peeking out beneath the baseball cap. His nose is broad, looking like it's been broken a few times, while freckles and pockmarks scar up his cheeks.

"Getting to know the neighbors already," he comments to her. He takes his sunglasses off, sliding them in the front pocket of his mustard yellow shirt, and gives me a steady look. His eyes are hazel, nearly amber, the kind of eyes that you know have seen a lot, been through a lot.

"Of course," Dawn says. She nods at me. "This is Ada. She lives here with her father." She lowers her voice. "She lost her mother a few years ago."

"What a shame," the man says frowning. "Death doesn't always discriminate, does it?" He offers his hand. "I'm Jacob. Family friend."

"Nice to meet you," I tell him, his hand nearly crushing mine.

The way he keeps his eyes on me is unnerving until he winks, breaking into a crooked smile. "It will be good for the Knightlys to have someone young next door, keep them breathing and all that." He takes his hand back and looks to Dawn. "Where is the husband anyway, napping? You know you should be careful, he's almost seventy.

Wouldn't want him to break his hip taking a shit or something."

She rolls her eyes. "You are terrible."

"That's why even Hell didn't want me," he jokes smoothly.

"Well he's already taken over the basement and turning it into a jam room. If he's breaking anything it's his back from hanging guitars all over the walls." Dawn gives me an apologetic look. "I best be showing Jacob the grand tour. This man doesn't know what patience is. Let me know how you like the brownies."

"Will do," I tell her, raising up the pan in a show of thanks.

"Come on Rusty," Jacob says, putting his arm around Dawn's shoulder and leading her to the house. "It's been a long drive. Take me to the gin."

I watch them disappear into the house before glancing down at the brownies. That whole exchange was kind of strange and there was definitely something odd about that redheaded fellow with the Michael Caine accent. I think I'll give the brownies to Dex, just in case. He can handle poison better than anyone.

I head inside the house, my dad puttering around in the kitchen trying to make dinner. I feel a pang of guilt knowing I should have been at home helping him instead of out buying makeup I don't need with money I don't have.

He doesn't even glance at the bags as I plop them on the counter. He stopped harassing me about spending money a long time ago. I think he figures I'm trying to shop my way out of grief just as he's taken up gardening tenfold. Even though we're trying to move, he spends most of the day out in the back garden. It looks so lush and extravagant now that you can't even tell it was once the

sight of a séance, a witch bottle filled with toenail clip-
pings and hair and all the negative energy of the house
buried there.

Then again, what backyard doesn't have that? It could
almost be a selling point.

"I met the neighbors," I tell him, sliding the pan on the
island. "Though I'm not sure if the brownies are poisoned
or not, so proceed with caution."

He glances at them briefly as he stoops to take a tray out
of the oven, the scent of roasted vegetables wafting out in a
cloud. "Oh. I met them earlier this morning." He starts
turning over the beets and carrots. "Interesting couple.
Turns out the man used to be in a seventies rock group,
though I can't say I've ever heard one of their songs. Your
sister would probably know. Or that husband of hers," he
mumbles under his breath.

"What band?"

"Hybrid? I can't remember. Something that would
induce a lot of drug use, I'm sure." A silence falls between
us, thick and uneasy. I know he's thinking about Perry when
she was younger. I know he's thinking about me last year.

I clear my throat. "Well that's good that they're cool," I
tell him. "Need any help? What time are they coming over
anyway?"

There's a brief knock at the door before we hear it open.
Dad sighs. "I suppose that's them."

"Hello?" Perry calls out from around the corner. She
comes into the kitchen and drops a giant duffle bag on the
floor that's nearly the size of her.

"You're here for a night, Perry," my dad chides her,
putting the vegetables back in the oven. "You've gotten just
as bad as Ada at packing."

"She wishes," I mumble before going over to Perry and

giving her a hug. I catch a whiff of cigarettes in her dark ponytail. "Ugh, have you taken up smoking?"

"No," she says exasperated as she pulls back. "Guess who thought he could smoke one cigarette and not get re-addicted?"

"My ears are burning!" comes Dex's voice from outside.

"No, that's your fucking cancer stick that's burning!" Perry yells right back. She looks back at me and shakes her head. "Asshole."

"Language, please," my father says, rolling his eyes before coming over and giving her a tight embrace. I'd just seen the two of them a few weeks ago when I went up to their place in a Seattle for a few nights, but my dad hasn't seen them in at least a month. And while he can do without seeing Dex, I know he misses Perry dearly.

She's looking good. Her weight fluctuates like most women's, though her giant boobs are always constant. I definitely wasn't blessed in that department. I may have inherited our mother's blonde hair and long limbs but Perry got all the sultry Italian curves from our dad's side. The only thing we really have in common are our sky blue eyes. Oh, and the whole seeing ghosts thing.

Which sucks.

"I've tried to get him onto E-cigarettes," Perry says to dad.

Dex's laugh comes loud and clear along with a waft of smoke, and I figure he's on the front steps finishing his cigarette.

"You want him to vape?" I ask Perry, raising my brow. "You might as well as staple the word 'shitdick' to his forehead."

"Ada," my dad admonishes me.

Dex laughs again and the front door closes. He appears

in the kitchen entryway, looking at Perry with raised brows. "You see? Only shitdicks vape. Your sister knows what's up."

"I always know what's up," I tell him dryly.

He shrugs, conceding, and nods at my father, tipping his newsboy cap at him. "Daniel."

"Dex," is his reply before he turns around to busy himself with more food.

"Can I help with anything?" Perry asks but our dad shoos us away.

"Go put your stuff away and relax," he says, opening the fridge. "Dinner will be ready in a half hour."

Dex scoops up Perry's bag, his large bicep muscles flexing beneath the sleeve of his grey tee shirt. He grins at me, wagging his brows and I immediately make a noise of disgust, looking away.

Okay, here's the truth about Declan "Dex" Foray. He bugs the absolute shit out of me, always has since he first waltzed into our lives all those years ago with his wannabe Robert Downey Jr. mustache and goatee and video camera. I thought he was here to exploit my sister, roping her into their YouTube channel as they investigated ghosts and the paranormal. Instead, he saved her. Changed her life in more ways than one. And I couldn't be happier that he's my brother-in-law now.

He also happens to be hot. I cringe when I find myself admitting it from time to time and I would *never* tell him or Perry that, lest his ego get even bigger than it is, but it's true. He's not exactly my type. I'm pretty tall and Dex is around 5'9", but there's still something about him that sets your heart aflutter sometimes. Maybe it's because he's ripped as shit, maybe it's his expressive dark eyes, the way he carries himself with so much "I don't give a shit" confidence. Or maybe it's that in some ways he's almost superhuman.

Could be anything, really.

But most of the time, he lives to annoy me, just like any brother would.

"Put your muscles away," I scoff at him as he brushes past, moving toward the staircase.

"Don't act like you don't like it, little sister," he calls over his shoulder, heading up the stairs.

"I think I liked it better when you called me Little Fifteen!" I yell after him. "Though I guess Little Eighteen doesn't have quite the same ring to it."

I step out into the hallway, about to head to the living room, when Perry intercepts me, putting her hand on my shoulder and squinting at me.

"Are you okay?" she asks softly.

"You think I'm offended because your husband is flexing for me?"

She frowns. "I'm serious. I hate to sound like a bitch, but you look awful."

I shrug away from her hand and go into the living room, flopping onto the couch and pulling out my phone to busy myself with fashion bloggers on Instagram. "I haven't been sleeping right."

She sits down beside me and I can feel her stare deepening as she leans in closer. I give her a quick glance. "Don't tell me you're going to try and read my mind. We had a deal."

She sits back, looking mildly embarrassed. "It doesn't work like that," she says in a clipped voice. "And you're right, we did have a deal."

I eye her warily. She says she can't just read my mind, though I'm pretty sure that's how she found out I lost my virginity to Dillon. In the backseat of his 1995 Toyota Tercel. Something I wish could be erased from my memory. Sadly there hasn't been anyone since him.

"I'm worried about you," she says after a moment, her voice quiet.

"Why?" I ask, afraid that she'll have all the good reasons.

She shrugs with one shoulder and looks down at her hands in her lap. "Just a feeling I have."

Perry and her *feelings*. It's never good news. She's never like, "I have a feeling we're going to win the lottery and you'll be swept off your feet by a charming billionaire." It's always "I have a feeling you're in danger and everyone around us is going to die."

Unfortunately, she's usually right about her feelings. She's always been intuitive, even when she was all screwed up, and ever since all her incidents—some of which have become my incidents—her intuition has doubled. That, along with her ability to project her thoughts into other's heads. She says she can't read minds in the same way but I just don't believe her. Sometimes I think about investing in a Magneto helmet around her when she starts pulling this Professor Xavier shit.

I sigh, wishing my heart wasn't starting to kick up a few notches. "What feeling?"

"I don't know. I'm having dreams," she says. "You're in them."

I swallow hard and look back down at the phone. "Anyone else in them?"

"No." She puts her hand on my knee until I look at her. Her eyes are rounder than ever as she stares at me. "You're having them too."

I quickly tuck my hair behind my ears. "It's nothing."

"Tell me about them."

"Tell me about yours," I counter. "Perhaps you'd better start from the beginning," I say, mimicking the opening lines of White Zombie's "Electric Head Pt. 1."

She exhales slowly. "Okay. Well I've been having them for the last two weeks."

Me too, I think.

"It's pretty much all the same. We're in the Thin Veil. Remember when we were there in New York?"

"You mean remember when I went to another dimension in the middle of Bryant Park to rescue you?" I repeat dryly. "Yeah. I remember, Perry."

"Right. Well it's like that, except it's on an island. It kind of reminds me of this island I was on once with Dex, you know where the lepers were."

"All your episodes kind of blur together," I tell her, motioning with my hand for her to speed it up.

"Anyway, you're standing on a cliff at the edge of the ocean. I'm down in a boat and I'm yelling up at you not to jump."

A shiver rocks through me.

She goes on. "And you stop just before you're about to go over. You listen to me. Then someone appears behind you. A shadow, a hand. And they push you."

"Great."

"You fall straight into the ocean and sink and I jump off the boat and swim for you." She pauses, biting her lip for a moment.

"And?" I coax her, knowing this ain't going to be good.

"You drown. No matter what, I can't get below the water to get you. I see you sink. And . . . well, you're not alone." My heart stills. "Mom is with you too."

I whistle slowly, breathing out. "Wow. I'm not sure what that means."

"Neither."

"Now I'm scared shitless."

"It's just a dream Ada, it doesn't *have* to mean anything. It's something my psyche is trying to work out."

I give her a levelling look. "We both know your psyche isn't normal. Especially if I'm having dreams too. Which, by the way, are nothing like yours. I just . . . well you know my exploding head syndrome?" She nods gravely and to her credit doesn't laugh at the name this time. "It's like that. I'm dreaming something is in my closet, then I hear the knocks and wake up. Or I'm with a guy but . . ."

"What guy?"

I shake my head. "I'm not really sure. Like, I have a feeling I know who he is but I don't really get a good look at him. It's almost like . . . Do you remember a guy at the wedding named Jay?"

I don't bother telling her that I thought I saw him today. One crazy thing at a time.

Her groomed brows pull together. "I remember you were drunk and walking around barefoot holding your heels in your hand and looking for a guy called Jay but that's it."

"So you don't remember inviting someone there by that name?"

She gives me a wry look. "Ada, I don't know who half the people there were. Ask dad, he's the one who went nuts with the guest list. Or Dex. A lot of people from his old work were invited. That whole day was such a blur."

"Ask me what?" Dex asks as he enters the room. He stops in front of us, folding his arms across his chest. "Am I interrupting girl time?"

"It's fine," Perry says. "Ada's been having strange dreams too."

Dex nods, sliding his fingers across the stubble on his jaw. "Well, I wouldn't worry about it. Ada is going off to school and our second wedding anniversary is coming up in October, which is enough to make any woman lose their shit. Two years as Mrs. Foray, it's a lot to handle."

"Tell me about it," Perry says under her breath, though there's a hint of a smile on her lips as she stares up at him. Lord, the two of them make me so sick sometimes with their love for each other. Sick and, I must admit, jealous.

Perry continues, "Did you know a guy at our wedding called Jay?"

Dex shakes his head, giving her a lopsided grin. "The only thing I knew that day was you, kiddo."

"Oh, barf," I say, sinking back into the couch.

He flashes his smile to me as he sits on the edge of the coffee table. "Sorry I'm not of any help. I guess we could go through the wedding photos. What's this all about? You hook up with him?"

"No," I say quickly, glaring at him. *I don't think so.* "I just feel like he's appearing in my dreams." I straighten up. "Anyway, weird dreams aside, I'm fine. Just . . ."

"On edge," Perry supplies.

"Well I am now since you told me you've been having feelings about things."

"Perry is always having feelings," Dex says. "It's usually her period's fault."

"Dex," she hisses at him. "Stop blaming everything on PMS."

He cocks a brow. "Right. Like you don't turn into a murderous she-devil once a month who plows through an entire cake even when you swear you're all gluten-free." He looks at me. "She makes me buy gluten-free bread for us. Have you ever tried that shit? It's like chewing on dried-out dogshit."

I raise my palm. "Stop. How would you even know what that tastes like?"

"Someone want to set the table?" Dad hollers from the kitchen.

Both Perry and I look expectantly at Dex. He can use the brownie points.

He sighs and gets up, trudging into the kitchen to get the plates.

I look back at Perry. "He's probably right you know."

"About the dried-out dogshit?"

"Yes. And also it being a stressful time of year for us. Me anyway. Maybe I'm just stressing and you're picking up on it and it's manifesting itself into dreams."

"You're nervous about starting school," she says sympathetically.

"Actually I'm excited. I just . . . you know. I wish mom was here for it."

Perry sighs and leans back into the cushions, running her hand over her face. "Yeah. I get it. I think of her during the stupidest times. Like, I'll pick up a pomegranate at the supermarket and think, would mom know what to do with this? I know I can Google it, but it's not the same. I just wish I could ask her advice on things, anything. Even though we weren't close, not like you guys, I thought—I knew—that in time we would grow closer."

My chest is weighted, the heavy hands of grief starting to climb up from the inside. Sometimes I forget that she and Perry weren't as close as we were. My mother treated her like the bad seed, the black sheep, because she was too afraid to see Perry for what she really was. When they finally began to reconcile . . . it was too late.

"I'm sorry," I say quietly, trying to keep my voice strong, even though we've talked about it many times before.

Perry's head lolls to the side and she smiles softly at me. "Don't be."

"Also, I don't want to move," I add.

"Still?" she asks, looking around the room. "I couldn't wait to get out of here. Aside from the fact that it's way too big for you and dad, doesn't this place scare you?"

"No," I tell her. Totally lying. Because this house *does* scare me. But at the same time, I feel compelled to stay here. It's not just because it's everything I've known, that I'm hanging onto memories of my mother. It's because it *needs* me to stay.

"All right ladies," Dex says poking his head around the corner. "Let's eat before your feelings turn to *hangriness*."

Dad made roast chicken and vegetables with mashed potatoes that he calls "special potatoes" even though the only thing that makes them special is the fact that there's bacon bits and truffle salt sprinkled in it. Well, that and they are damn good.

We gather around the table, helping ourselves to the food and conversation that doesn't involve feelings and dreams and death.

"Hey I saw you have new neighbors now," Dex says between mouthfuls of chicken. "Poor people don't know who they've moved next door to." His brows raise at Perry. "Had they moved in a few years ago, they wouldn't have lasted long with all the shenanigans and whatnot."

Shenanigans. What a simple way to describe everything that went down here.

"Actually," I tell him, "I met the woman today. She's

really nice. They're old though." My dad coughs on purpose and I shrug. "Sorry, *older*. Retired. And apparently the husband was in a '70s rock band."

Dex cocks his head. "What band?"

"Hybrid?" my father says before taking a sip of wine.

"Holy fuck!" Dex exclaims, pressing his hands down onto the table, his dark brown eyes looking half-crazed. "Are you shitting me?"

"Who is Hybrid?" I ask, looking between him and Perry.

"They were massive back in the day," Perry explains. "Totally influenced Kyuss, Melvins, and Queens of the Stone Age. Sounds a bit like Black Sabbath. Weird shit went down with that band."

"Who is the guy, do you know?" Dex asks eagerly.

My dad shrugs while I say, "I didn't get his name. But the woman's name is Dawn. Dawn Knightly."

Now he's even more impressed. "Holy shit."

"Dex," my dad warns him.

"Look, *dad*," Dex says. "I'm thirty-five years old and I can say holy fucking shit if I want to."

My dad glares at him.

I can tell Perry is trying to kick Dex under the table. "That might be true but don't forget my dad—*our* dad—is a theology professor."

"Who is Dawn Knightly?" I ask, attempting to breakup their showdown which happens every time we all get together. "Was she in the band?"

Dex tears his eyes away from my dad's death stare and looks at me in such a way that I know I'm about to get an earful. "No. She was the music journalist who Sage Knightly, the guitarist, fell in love with. Documented the rise and fall of the band on their last tour before everything went to hell in a handbasket. You want to talk about infamous tours, that one is for the books. There's a whole mythology built around it, which now I wonder if it could have been real after all." He leans back in his chair, taking off his cap and running his hand through his thick black hair, eyes going to the door. "Damn. I wonder if I should go over and introduce myself."

"And say what?" I ask. "Ask him for his autograph?"

He gives me a withering glance. "Sage Knightly had a bunch of solo albums after Hybrid. I wonder if he could give me permission to use some of his music in my documentary. Fuck knows the Deftones will never respond to me."

"Will you ever tell us what the documentary is about?" my father asks gruffly. "You've been talking about it for ages now."

After Dex and Perry called it quits with their Experiment in Terror YouTube show (*they* were the original YouTubers), they were both at a loss of what to do with themselves. Luckily it didn't take them long to figure it out. I thought that they might go the paranormal investigator route much like the Warrens (you know, the real life couple *The Conjuring* was based on), but they seem to have put everything scary behind them. For now, anyway. Can't say I blame them.

Instead they opened up a company together, Haunted Media. Dex uses his prowess as an editor, cameraman, and musician to make music videos for some major artists. I never thought you could turn making music videos into a career, especially in the age where MTV plays nothing but the Kardashians, but Dex has a dark and creepy tone to his work that goes over well with so many bands and artists. Perry is the manager of the company, the brains and the beauty. She keeps Dex in line, which he needs badly, and is the key liaison between the business and the customers. The saying *behind every man is a great woman,* is totally true in this case.

But then there's this documentary that Dex keeps mentioning but never tells anyone what it's about. Even Perry shrugs when I ask. I know he has aspirations to be a legit filmmaker beyond the music video business, so a documentary makes the most sense as a stepping stone, but he's always been strangely cagey about it. Then again, Dex is a pretty cagey guy by nature, so I don't read too much into it.

"You'll find out once I know," Dex says and I know he won't give us anything more than that.

After dinner I head up to my room to work on my blog for a little bit, which means going through and editing a slew of photos I took with Amy and Tom last week. I admit, I've been slacking on my blogging duties which isn't good since that's really the whole reason I got into my design school. They liked my sketches of course, but it was the whole social media aspect of being a fashion blogger and the fact that I've had my blog since I was fifteen that helped seal the deal. They wanted to take on someone who already had a personal brand and a platform to move forward with.

Perry and Dex are downstairs watching a movie on Netflix and even though I'm working on my sketches, trying my hardest to get the right forms for a leather jacket— maybe a leather jacket partially inspired by the one I thought I saw today, the one belonging to the man who may or may not exist—but I just can't get it right.

I guess I doze off with my head on the sketchpad and a charcoal pencil in my hand.

Three hard knocks seem to ricochet through my brain.

CHAPTER THREE

My head snaps up from my desk and I let out a muffled cry, heart bouncing in my chest as I try and rescue my thoughts from sleep.

I pull off the paper that's stuck to my cheek and quickly look around. My bedroom is dark except for the light above my desk. I'm alone, though I could have sworn those three knocks came from someone pounding on the desk, beside my head. That's how much it rattled me.

I try and catch my breath, taking air in deep and slow. I reach for my phone to check the time, wondering how long I've been asleep, wondering if Perry and Dex are still down-stairs watching TV, when there's a flutter at the window.

I gasp and whirl around, nearly falling out of my chair.

Something black flashes past outside the window, the light's reflection on the glass obscuring most of it.

Holy shit.

I'm on the second floor but that doesn't really matter because once upon a time, Perry saw a demon on the roof and then fell off said roof trying to run from it. I could never figure out why she even went out there but now I know.

Complete morbid curiosity.

I slowly get out of my chair and edge toward the window, heart in my throat, watching my reflection get closer as I approach it. I reach for the window edge to open it the rest of the way.

I'm just about to open it when an intense chill runs over my limbs, like someone's just dumped a bucket of ice water down my arms and back.

A slow, laborious *creak* comes from behind me.

From the closet.

I freeze.

Suddenly the window doesn't seem so interesting anymore.

Bony fingers of terror skitter down my spine and I'm turning around.

The closet door is open a few inches even though I know it was closed before.

Maybe it was the wind, I tell myself.

There is no wind. If anything, the room has become still, like all the air and smell and life has been sucked out of it and the only thing left is dust.

Maybe I'm dreaming.

I'm always dreaming.

With that in mind, my feet start moving across the room, the rug cold on my soles. I'm poised, every nerve in my body ready to spring, my heart beating so fast I swear it has wings.

I stop outside the closet door and stare dumbly at the crack. The space taunts me with the dark depths behind it. In this moment it feels like it's not a closet at all, instead it's something infinite. A doorway to something horrible.

My hand slowly reaches for the doorknob.

I pause, my hand shaking, losing all nerve to grab it.

Then . . .

"Help me, Ada," a faint voice rasps from inside the closet.

The voice of my mother.

The light in the closet goes on.

I scream.

My whole body launches backward and I'm running for the door out of my room and into the hallway.

I run right into Dex.

"Ada," he says, grabbing my shoulders. "What is it, what happened?"

My mouth flaps open, soundless as I stare at him and then Perry as she appears behind him, coming out of my old bedroom.

"Something is in my closet," I manage to say, my whole body trembling now.

The door at the end of the hall opens and my dad stares at us, slipping on his robe and sliding his glasses down on his face.

"It's past midnight. What's going on?" he says gruffly, voice hoarse from sleep.

I look up at Dex, not sure what to say.

"She had a dream," Perry says to him quickly. "It's nothing. Go back to sleep, dad."

We stand there in the hallway, halfway to my room, watching my dad carefully. Thankfully he takes the bait, even though I know, I *know* I wasn't sleeping this time. He frowns at me with a mix of exasperation and concern on his face before stepping back inside his room.

"Stay behind me," Dex says, pushing me so Perry and I are behind him. Like hell I'd want to go back in first.

Dex walks to the middle of my room while Perry and I hang around the doorway.

"This closet?" Dex asks, pointing at it. It's still open a crack though the light is off now. "I only ask because it feels like Perry and I are sleeping in an extension of your closet too."

"Yes," I tell him, too afraid to be annoyed. "But the light was on. It turned on, *by itself,* just as I was about to open the door. I heard . . ." I trail off, not sure if I should say anything else.

Perry is watching me closely. "Heard what?"

I swallow hard and give her a pleading look. "I heard mom," I whisper.

"You know that's not her," she says to me but I can't quite agree.

Dex frowns at us, then looks around him. He quickly moves to the desk and grabs the pencil I was using to sketch and holds it like a knife.

"What the hell are you going to do with that?" Perry hisses. "Draw the ghosts?"

He tilts his head, giving her an incredulous look. "Have you ever been stabbed with a pencil in the eye? No, because if you had, you'd probably be dead. Anyway, no one said anything about ghosts."

"No one has to say anything about ghosts," I say. "But I don't think this is that. I know when I'm dealing with a ghost and when I'm dealing with . . . well, I don't know. If I'm not dreaming then I'm going fucking crazy."

Perry quickly pinches my arm, hard.

"Ow! The fuck?" I cry out, shying away from her.

"Not dreaming."

Dex takes in a deep breath and whips the closet door open.

My hands fly to my face. I don't know what I'm expecting.

But it's empty. Just full of my clothes, shirts hanging from the rattling hangers. Dex stoops, sticking his hands into the bottom of the closet, shuffling through sandals and heels and clothes that have fallen.

"There's nothing," he says, straightening up. "Except that you have an obscene amount of heels that belong on a stripper named Candy."

"Shut the fuck up," I tell him, glaring.

He raises his palms, walking over to us. "Hey, I've known some mighty fine strippers in my day. It's not an insult. Unless your name is Candy."

Perry rolls her eyes. "I thought you were fond of the ones called Marla."

"Ah, you remember," he says happily.

Perry ignores him and turns to me. "So what exactly happened?"

I point at the desk. "I was sketching and fell asleep. I woke up. I heard the knocks."

"Good ol' exploding head syndrome," Dex comments.

"Yes. That. But I swear it was right here, like someone was pounding on the desk. Of course I woke up and I was alone. Then there was something outside the window."

Dex walks over to the window and hauls it up, sticking his head out for a moment.

"There's a giant ass bird in the tree right there," he says. "Could it be that? Looks like a raven."

"Oh, well there just happens to be a fucking raven outside my window, can't mean a thing," I tell him, coming over.

I peer outside and sure enough, there's a raven sitting at the end of the tree, its silhouette lit up by the streetlights. It cocks its head at me, staring at me with beady, glassy eyes, then flies off, its wings beating heavily as it goes.

I shudder again. There aren't a lot of ravens around here, only crows. And I've certainly never seen any past midnight, nor hanging around the tree outside my window.

"Ignoring the bird for now," Dex says, though from the hard look in his eyes I know he's thinking something of it too, "then what happened?"

"I heard the closet door open. It wasn't open before. It was closed. I swear it. Then I went toward it."

"As you do when you think there's something horrible in your closet," Dex says.

"And then I heard my mom's voice. She said, help me,

Ada." I look at Perry with wide-eyes. "It was her. I know it was her. She sounded so far away, so . . . strained. Then the light went on and I screamed and ran."

Perry and Dex exchange a look.

"What?" I ask.

"Nothing," Perry says, coming over to me. She puts her hand on my shoulder and gives it a squeeze. "Want to sleep with us tonight?"

I wrinkle my nose. "No thanks. You do believe me, don't you?"

"Of course we believe you," Perry says. "You could tell me my old stuffed animals are trying to kill you and I'd believe you."

"Wait, what?" I ask, my eyes flitting to the bed where I know her stuffed animals are stored in a box underneath.

"But I also think you're stressed and exhausted and liable to seeing things. I know sometimes when I was seeing shit it wasn't because there were actual ghosts, I was just so on edge that everything seemed out to get me." She looks at Dex. "Sorry baby, I'm sleeping with my sister tonight."

He shrugs. "Suit yourself. You girls need anything, you know where I am." He leaves the room, stretching his arms over his head. "Love you," he calls over his shoulder. "You too, Perry."

She raises her brow in mild amusement and looks back to me.

"You don't have to stay here," I tell her.

"You've done the same for me before," she says. She looks around her. "Though honestly this isn't my favorite place to be." She climbs into the bed, moving to the other side. For a moment I'm transported back two years when Perry still lived here, our mother was still alive and things, at least for me, were more or less normal.

But my brain won't let me pretend for long. Even though Perry is still just twenty-five and looks pretty much the same as she did, there's a world-weariness to her eyes, the kind that old souls have, the kind that says she's seen too much and can never go back to the way she was.

I quickly get changed into my matching camisole and boy-short set and get in bed beside her, feeling like a little girl again under the covers.

I turn over on the pillow to look at her. "You know what this reminds me of? When we used to go to the cabin when we were little."

She rolls over to face me, folding up the thin pillow underneath her head. "Was this when you said I had an imaginary friend and I'd go and talk to him through the window every night?"

"But he never was imaginary, was he?"

She shakes her head, frowning. "No. Nothing ever is." She closes her eyes. "Nothing ever is."

You'd think it would be impossible for both of us to sleep, but in seconds she's out like a light.

Then I follow.

~

I'm dreaming.

For once, I know it.

And I know exactly where I am.

I'm in the Thin Veil, a place I've only been to once and here I am again; here but not.

The world is both red and grey, a desaturated hue that seeps into everything, my hands, my clothes, the crunchy, dead grass beneath me.

I'm sitting on a cliff overlooking the ocean, much like

the one Perry had mentioned earlier, the one in her dreams. Only she's nowhere to be found. There's only the empty sea with waves crashing below, faraway islands in the distance. There is a forest of fir and hemlock behind me, a dark, seemingly fathomless thicket.

Hi.

I whip my head around to see a man, *the* man, the leather jacket wearing ginger who may or may not be a man named Jay, standing over me.

I stare up at his hulking body, no jacket this time, just a plain t-shirt that shows off every taut muscle, and jeans. He gives me a half-smile.

Mind if I sit down?

He's speaking to me, right into my head, without opening his mouth.

I'm not a fan of this.

I open my mouth and am surprised when the words, "Can I talk?" come out.

"Of course," he says. "I understand it must be strange for you. It's still strange for me."

I frown at him. My dreams have been so lucid lately, but never the ones that have involved him. I've never been able to just exist like this, to interact with him and have it be so real.

I need to take advantage.

"Who are you?" I ask him. "I mean, I know I'm dreaming."

He stares down at me, his smile twisting slightly. My god, this dude is even more handsome up close. I'm starting to think there is no way in hell that I met him in real life because if he really was the guy from the wedding, I know I would have remembered every detail of his face, no matter how blackout drunk I got.

"*Are* you dreaming?" he asks, easing himself down to sit beside me. He props his elbows on his knees and gives me a sidelong glance. "Or are you awake?"

All the hairs on my arm stand up and I can't tell if it's because he's so close or the way his eyes seem to gaze right into the heart of me, or because I'm starting to think maybe I am awake after all.

"You never answered my question," I tell him, shifting away slightly, his proximity to me producing a strange push pull, like two magnets about to connect. "Why do I keep dreaming you? Have we met before? What's your name?"

"So many questions, Ada, so little time" he says. There's something so soothing about his voice, both low and silken, even in such a dead place like this where all sound is worn down, dull. "But you have met me before. At the wedding."

"I knew it," I whisper, feeling mildly triumphant.

"I guess it doesn't say much about me that you don't really remember," he says with a wince, a piece of wavy hair flopping on his forehead. "Or maybe it says a lot."

"I blame the champagne," I tell him. "So now I know I've met you before. Am I conjuring you up because I found you absurdly handsome and I'm hoping to pick up where we left off?"

Okay, normally I'm not this forward with guys but it's my dream, I can do what the hell I want.

The corner of his mouth quirks up. He has damn fine lips. "We didn't really leave off anywhere. You took off your shoes and went to get champagne. I never saw you again."

I'm wondering if that's true or if it's what my subconscious wants me to believe. After all, it's pretty much what Perry had told me earlier.

"You're here," he says slowly, his face falling slightly, "because I have something to show you."

He gets to his feet in one fluid motion and reaches down for my hand.

Without thinking, as if my hand has a mind of its own, it goes to his and I feel an immediate jolt of electricity running through me. Not just the electricity you read about in romance novels. I mean actual voltage. My lips are buzzing.

"Sorry," he says, hauling me to my feet, still holding onto my hand. "The connection in here can be a livewire."

A livewire? It's magnetic is what it is, it feels like my palm is stuck to his and our hands meld together like they were always meant to be this way.

Fuck. Though the respite from the horror is welcome, I'm not sure all this Twilight-like, magnetic, electric bullshit is any better, dream-wise.

Come on, he says in my head. *And use your inside voice.*

Okay, I say, hearing my words escape, despite not opening my mouth.

He leads the way, his large form in front of me as he takes me toward the forest.

The forest of darkness and death.

My chest feels heavy and he pauses, looking at me over his shoulder.

You'll be fine with me. I won't let anything happen to you.

What are you showing me? I ask him. *I don't even really know who you are.*

I'm the one who has your back, he says. *And I've been watching you for a very, very long time.*

I don't have the luxury to puzzle over his remark. We enter the forest and I immediately feel this sense of doom slide over me, as if evil has taken up residence here and it's just oozing from the trees. The light in here is nearly gone and I can barely make out the tree trunks from the shadows.

Everything is the darkest, grainiest red, a world seeped in blood.

Without realizing it, I'm holding his hand for dear life. He's leading me further into my nightmare and I don't even know his name.

It's Jay, he says, glancing at me over his shoulder.

Oh great, Jay, the thought reader.

Sorry, he says. *It's impossible not to when we're in here.*

You keep saying in here, I say as I give wide berth to a flowering vine that's reaching halfway across the path. I swear there are eyeballs at the center of the flowers, watching me as I go. *You mean my dream.*

He doesn't say anything for a moment. *Things aren't always as they seem here.*

No shit, I mutter to myself.

Suddenly he stops and I run into his back. A nice, hard, firm back. I yearn to run my fingers over his muscles and reach up to do so, because again, it's my dream and it's been forever since I've had a sexy one, but he says, *listen.*

I take my hand away, my other still grasping his, unable to let go, and cock my head in concentration.

I hear a flurry of wings beating and look up to see the faint shape of what looks to be a bat the size of an eagle flying overhead, a black blot beyond the dark reaches of the tree limbs.

Not that, he says.

I close my eyes, straining to hear more.

At first I just hear my own heartbeat, a strange thing to pick up on in a dream, and for a moment I wonder if I'm still in bed with Perry, if my heart is racing in real life, if I'm tossing and turning.

Then I hear it.

Again.

"Help me, Ada."

My mother's voice.

I grasp Jay's hand tighter. *What is that? What's going on?*

It's not your mother, he says, glancing down at me, his brows low. *That's what I want to show you, what you need to know.*

I peer around him.

The path in front of us widens, but as the trees fan out, it doesn't become lighter. It becomes darker. Instead of a forest it's a black veil, like we're standing on the edge of a starless universe. And there, just feet away in the earth, is a large gaping pit with a sole hand sticking out of it.

I know without a doubt that it's my mother's hand. I know her hand. I feel her near, a connection that can't be broken.

I start for it but Jay pulls me back, his hand going to my elbow and taking a firm hold.

It's not your mother, he warns.

Help me, my mother cries out, her voice soft and ragged all at once, like she's barely holding onto life.

Even though she's dead.

Please, I tell him, trying to wrestle free from his grasp. *She needs me.*

My mother screams bloody murder, her hand gripping the side of the hole, fingers digging into dirt, barely holding on.

I know you're there, you can save me, she gasps. *You need to save my soul. They have me and won't let me go.*

"I'm trying!" I yell, wishing I could see her face, wanting to grab her hand and pull her up.

Shhh, Jay hushes me, eyes blazing into me as his grip tightens. *They might know.*

More giant bats start flying overhead, one landing a few feet from my mother's grasping hand.

Who might know? I cry out in frustration. *It's a fucking dream and I'm either saving my mom or I'm waking up.*

I won't let you, he says. *This isn't over.*

I stare at him incredulously. *Won't let me?*

He points at what I can only assume is the pit to hell. *That is not real. That isn't your mother. This is what I had to show you, why I had to show you myself.*

Of course it isn't real, I snap, my chest heavy, as if loaded with bricks. *It's a dream.*

Listen, Jay says, placing his large hands on my shoulders, an iron grip to keep me in place. He lowers his head, his eyes inches from mine and searching. *And listen carefully. No matter what happens, you mustn't believe your mother is in any danger. She's dead and she's safe.*

That's an oxymoron if I ever heard one, I mutter, trying to ignore my mother's cries, even though they stab deep, like hot knives.

Whatever it is, she's okay. Don't attempt to seek her out. Don't attempt to interfere.

How can I interfere?

Let it be and ignore it.

I think I'd really like to wake up now. I look around, staring at the darkness. "Wake up, wake up, WAKE UP!" I scream.

"Shhhh!" Jay hushes me. "I'm not supposed to be here with you."

A dozen more giant bats land on the earth around us with soft thumps.

Jay looks over his shoulder at them and then back at me.

He gives me a small shake of his head. "You need to go to sleep now."

Knock.

Knock.

Knock.

Three knocks reverberate through the air.

In a flash I'm sucked backward through darkness, Jay, the bats, the forest growing smaller and disappearing.

Suddenly I'm back at home.

Standing downstairs in the kitchen.

In the dark.

I gasp for air, as if I haven't been breathing this whole time, and lean against the island for support, my legs suddenly going weak. A wave of nausea rolls through me and I barely have time to make it to the sink before I vomit. I stay hunched over, trying to get through it, catching my breath, until I have enough strength to get a glass from the cupboard.

Grimacing, I rinse my vomit down the sink then splash water on my face before filling my glass from the tap and downing it. I am beyond thirsty even after that and have to fill it again.

When I'm done, I push the glass away and look around the kitchen warily. I'm in my camisole and short shorts, barefoot, and yet I feel like I've spent the last few hours trudging through a forest.

It was a dream, I tell myself. *A bad one.*

And now I'm apparently sleepwalking. That's a new one for me.

I take in a deep breath and absently walk over to the window that looks out onto the street.

The air leaves my lungs.

There's a man standing in the middle of the road.

His form dark and faceless against the streetlights.

I freeze, wide-eyed, watching him.

I feel him watching me.
Neither of us move.
Then he turns and walks away.
Goes right next door.
To our new neighbors, the Knightlys'.